The Vampire Within

By Bradley Shadows
Copyright 2024
By Bradley Shadows

Chapter 1: The Return

The road to Sinclair Manor was longer than Elena remembered. It had been years since she last traveled the winding, fog-covered path through the dense forests that surrounded her family's estate. As her old car bumped along the gravel road, she could see the tops of the spires of the house peeking through the trees, stark and cold against the gloomy sky.

The message had come three days ago: her father, Nathaniel Sinclair, was dead. There were no details—just a letter from a solicitor, brief and formal, informing her of his passing and asking her to come and settle his affairs.

Elena hadn't spoken to her father in years. Their relationship had crumbled when she was barely a teenager, her mother's sudden death driving a wedge between them that never healed. He had retreated into himself, into the dark halls of Sinclair Manor, leaving Elena to grow up alone in the world. Her mother's side of the family had taken her in, raising her far from the secrets of her father's home.

Now, as she approached the estate, the memories came rushing back. The sprawling, gothic mansion had always unsettled her, even as a child. Its tall, arched windows seemed to peer down at her like eyes, watching her every move. The wind howled through the trees, carrying with it the eerie creaks and groans of the old house settling into its age.

She parked the car and stepped out into the cool autumn air, her boots crunching on the gravel. The manor loomed ahead, a dark silhouette against the darkening sky. Elena took a deep breath, trying to steady her nerves. She hadn't expected to feel so uneasy, but something about the place felt... wrong.

The front door was as heavy as she remembered. It groaned on its hinges as she pushed it open, revealing the grand, but neglected, foyer. Dust motes swirled in the air, catching the last fading rays of sunlight that streamed through the high windows. The smell of damp and decay greeted her, mingling with the faint scent of old books and leather.

"Hello?" Elena's voice echoed through the empty house, but there was no response.

She stepped inside, her footsteps muted by the thick layer of dust on the floor. The house was just as she had left it all those years ago—silent, foreboding, and full of shadows. A large portrait of her father hung above the fireplace in the drawing room, his eyes cold and distant, just as she remembered them. She shuddered and looked away.

Her father's study was on the second floor, at the end of a long hallway lined with portraits of her ancestors. Their eyes seemed to follow her as she walked, the weight of her family's past pressing down on her. She stopped in front of the door to the study, her hand hovering over the brass doorknob. For a moment, she hesitated, the weight of years of estrangement between her and her father pressing down on her chest.

With a deep breath, she turned the knob and pushed the door open.

The study was dimly lit, the curtains drawn tightly across the tall windows. Her father's large mahogany desk sat in the center of the room, papers strewn across its surface as though he had been working on something just moments before his death. A glass of amber liquid—whiskey, no doubt—still sat untouched beside the desk, the faint scent of it lingering in the air.

Elena walked slowly around the room, her fingers brushing over the spines of the old books that lined the walls. Many of them were written in languages she didn't recognize, their titles faded and worn from age. Her father had always been a scholar, obsessed with his work, but she had never known exactly what that work was.

On the desk, among the scattered papers, lay an old leather-bound journal. The cover was worn, its pages yellowed with age. Elena picked it up, her fingers tracing the intricate design on the front. Her father's handwriting, neat and precise, filled the pages. It was a diary of sorts, but it was far from ordinary.

The entries detailed his descent into madness—at least, that's what it seemed like at first. He wrote of shadows that moved on their own, of strange voices calling to him from the darkness, and of a curse that had plagued their family for generations. Elena's heart raced as she flipped through the pages, her eyes scanning the increasingly frantic writing.

Then, one sentence stopped her cold.

The curse of the vampire runs through our bloodline.

She stared at the words, her mind reeling. A vampire curse? It had to be a joke, a figment of her father's unraveling mind. But as she read on, the details became more and more specific. He wrote of an ancient ancestor, a deal made with a creature of the night, and the bloodline that had been tainted ever since.

Elena slammed the journal shut, her hands trembling. It was absurd. Vampires weren't real. Her father had clearly lost his mind, driven mad by isolation and whatever dark thoughts had haunted him in this old house.

But a small voice in the back of her mind whispered otherwise. The strange dreams she had been having, the inexplicable sensations that had begun to plague her over the past few weeks—they suddenly took on a more sinister meaning.

She stood abruptly, the journal clutched tightly in her hands. She needed answers, and there was only one person who could give them to her.

Dr. Victor Lennox.

Chapter 2: Shadows of the Past

Dr. Victor Lennox had always been a family friend, though Elena hadn't seen him in years. He was a man of science, a respected professor of biology who had once been close to her father. If anyone knew what Nathaniel had been working on—or if there was any truth to the madness in his journal—it would be Lennox.

The next morning, Elena found herself driving to Lennox's home, a small cottage on the outskirts of town. The road was quiet, the same fog clinging to the trees as it had the night before. The sun struggled to break through the overcast sky, casting the landscape in muted shades of gray.

She hadn't called ahead. She wasn't even sure if Lennox still lived there, but she had no other choice. Her father's journal had left her shaken, and the strange sensations in her body were growing stronger. She couldn't ignore the fact that something was happening to her.

Lennox's cottage came into view, a quaint stone house covered in ivy. She parked the car and walked up the cobblestone path, her nerves buzzing with anticipation. She knocked on the door and waited.

A moment later, the door creaked open, revealing the familiar face of Dr. Lennox. He was older now, his hair graying at the temples, but his sharp blue eyes were as piercing as ever. He looked surprised to see her.

"Elena?" he asked, his voice tinged with disbelief. "What are you doing here?"

"I need to talk to you," she said, her voice more urgent than she intended. "It's about my father."

Lennox's expression darkened, and he stepped aside, gesturing for her to come in. The inside of the cottage was just as she remembered—warm, inviting, and cluttered with books and papers. He led her to a small sitting room, where a fire crackled in the hearth.

"What's going on?" he asked once they were seated. "I heard about Nathaniel. I'm sorry for your loss."

Elena nodded, not trusting herself to speak for a moment. She pulled the journal from her bag and handed it to Lennox. "Have you ever seen this?"

Lennox took the journal, his brow furrowing as he flipped through the pages. His eyes widened as he read, and when he finally looked up at her, his face was pale.

"Elena," he said slowly, "where did you find this?"

"In my father's study," she replied. "What does it mean? Is it true?"

Lennox was silent for a long moment, his gaze fixed on the journal in his hands. Finally, he sighed and set it aside. "Your father and I... we were working on something—something that shouldn't have been possible."

"What are you talking about?" Elena asked, her heart pounding in her chest.

"It's true," Lennox said, his voice low. "Your family... the Sinclair bloodline... it's cursed. Vampirism isn't just a myth, Elena. It's real."

Chapter 3: The Awakening

Elena sat in stunned silence, trying to process what Dr. Lennox had just told her. Vampires were real? And her family was cursed with this ancient bloodline? It sounded impossible, absurd. But deep down, something told her it was true. Her father's journal wasn't just the ramblings of a madman—it was a record of something far more dangerous.

"How is that even possible?" she finally asked, her voice hoarse with disbelief. "Vampires… they're just stories, myths."

Lennox leaned forward, his blue eyes piercing her with their intensity. "That's what most people believe, but the myths come from somewhere. Your ancestor, Lucius Sinclair, made a pact centuries ago with a creature—an ancient vampire. It was supposed to bring him power and immortality, but like all deals of that nature, it came with a cost."

"What kind of cost?" Elena asked, dread creeping into her veins.

"The vampire's bloodline would merge with his own," Lennox explained. "Every descendant of Lucius Sinclair has carried that bloodline within them, dormant. But it's not always so dormant. In some, like your father, it begins to manifest—slowly at first, then more aggressively. He was fighting it, Elena. That's what his research was about. He was trying to find a way to stop the curse from taking him."

Elena's heart raced as she recalled the strange sensations she'd been experiencing recently—the heightened senses, the vivid dreams of blood, and the growing hunger she couldn't explain. "You mean… this is happening to me, too?"

Lennox's gaze softened. "I'm afraid so. The symptoms you're feeling—they're the early stages of the transformation. You've inherited the curse, Elena. And now, the vampire within you is starting to awaken."

She felt a chill run down her spine. It was all too much to take in—the sudden death of her estranged father, the discovery of a cursed bloodline, and now this. "There has to be a way to stop it," she said, her voice trembling. "My father—did he find anything?"

Lennox sighed deeply, running a hand through his graying hair. "Your father was close, but he ran out of time. The transformation overtook him before he could complete his research. But there may still be hope. He left behind notes, experiments, ideas that could help you."

Elena swallowed hard. "And what happens if I… if I don't stop it?"

Lennox didn't look away, but his face grew grim. "If the transformation completes, you'll lose control. The vampire side will take over, and you'll no longer be yourself. You'll be driven by hunger and instinct, no different from the creatures in the old stories."

She felt the weight of his words like a heavy stone sinking in her chest. The idea of losing herself, of becoming some kind of monster, terrified her. But there was something else too—a part of her, deep down, that wasn't just afraid. It was… curious.

Before she could stop herself, the question escaped her lips. "What's it like?"

Lennox raised an eyebrow. "What do you mean?"

"To be… to be like them. To have that kind of power."

There was a long silence before Lennox responded. "It's intoxicating," he said finally, his voice low and cautious. "That's why it's so dangerous. The power can consume you. The more you give in to it, the harder it becomes to turn back."

Elena shivered. She didn't want to be consumed, but the idea of wielding such power, of being more than human—it was tempting, even if she didn't want to admit it.

"Is there anyone else like me?" she asked, trying to push the dangerous thoughts aside. "Anyone who's been through this?"

"There have been others," Lennox said, his expression unreadable. "Most of them… didn't survive the transformation. But there is one who did."

Elena's eyes snapped to his. "Who?"

Lennox hesitated, then said a name that made her blood run cold. "The Elder Vampire."

She recoiled at the mention of the name. The Elder Vampire—the creature responsible for her family's curse. The one who had started all of this.

"He's still alive?" Elena asked, her voice barely a whisper.

Lennox nodded. "If you can call it living. He's ancient—older than any human civilization. He's been in hiding for centuries, but I believe he's still out there. If anyone knows how to break the curse, it would be him."

Elena felt a surge of fear and resolve. "How do I find him?"

Lennox shook his head. "You don't. You stay away from him, Elena. He's dangerous beyond measure. If you go looking for him, you might not come back."

But even as Lennox warned her, Elena couldn't help but feel that finding the Elder Vampire might be her only chance. If her father's research wasn't enough, then she needed to go to the source.

"I'll think about it," she said, standing up. "Thank you, Dr. Lennox. I need to go."

Lennox looked at her with concern, but he didn't try to stop her. "Be careful, Elena. This path... it's not one you can walk lightly."

She nodded and left the cottage, her mind swirling with the revelations of the day. The curse of the Sinclair family was real, and it was happening to her. But the question that haunted her as she drove back to the estate was not just whether she could stop it.

It was whether she *wanted* to.

Chapter 4: The Hunger

That night, Elena couldn't sleep. She lay in her old childhood bed, staring up at the ceiling as her thoughts churned restlessly. Her body ached with an odd, feverish sensation, as though her very blood was changing inside her. The more she tried to ignore it, the worse it became.

Eventually, she couldn't take it anymore. She threw off the covers and got out of bed, pacing the length of the room. Her skin felt too tight, her senses too sharp. Every sound seemed amplified—the creak of the floorboards, the rustle of the wind outside, the distant hum of the night creatures in the woods.

But it wasn't just the sounds. It was something else—something deeper, more primal.

Hunger.

It gnawed at her insides, an insistent, relentless craving that she didn't understand. At first, she thought it was just nerves, or maybe the lingering effects of her conversation with Lennox. But as the hours passed, the hunger only grew stronger.

She stumbled into the bathroom and splashed cold water on her face, trying to calm herself down. But when she looked up into the mirror, she didn't recognize the face staring back at her.

Her eyes—normally a soft green—were now rimmed with red, the irises glowing faintly in the dim light. Her skin looked pale, almost translucent, and her lips were slightly parted, revealing the faintest hint of sharp teeth.

Elena backed away from the mirror in horror, her heart pounding in her chest. She clutched the edge of the sink, trying to steady herself, but the hunger roared inside her, demanding to be fed.

She couldn't stay in the house. Not like this.

Grabbing her jacket, she fled out the door and into the night, the cold air hitting her like a slap. She ran down the driveway, past the towering trees that lined the path to the estate. The forest loomed ahead, dark and foreboding, but she didn't care. All she could think about was the hunger—the need to satisfy it, to make it stop.

Her senses guided her through the woods, her feet moving faster than she thought possible. The world around her blurred as she sprinted, her body moving with an unnatural speed. She could smell the damp earth, the scent of animals nearby, the rustle of leaves in the wind. And beneath it all, she could smell something else—something warm, pulsing, alive.

Blood.

Elena stopped abruptly; her breath ragged. She could hear it now—the sound of a heartbeat, slow and steady. It was close. Too close.

Without thinking, she followed the sound, her body moving on instinct. The heartbeat grew louder as she approached, and soon she saw the source—a deer, grazing quietly in the moonlit clearing.

The hunger surged within her, and before she could stop herself, she lunged.

Her hands grabbed the deer's neck, her teeth sinking into its flesh. The warm blood flooded her mouth, and she drank deeply, her mind clouded with the sheer pleasure of it. The hunger began to fade, replaced by a rush of power that filled every fiber of her being.

When she finally pulled away, the deer lay limp in her arms, its life drained away. Elena stared down at the animal in horror, blood staining her lips and hands. She dropped the body and stumbled back, wiping her mouth with the back of her hand, but the taste of blood lingered.

What had she done?

Her stomach churned with revulsion, but at the same time, she felt... stronger. More alive. The hunger had been sated, and for the first time in days, she felt a strange sense of calm.

But the calm was fleeting, replaced by a deep, gnawing fear.

She had tasted blood. And she had liked it.

Chapter 5: The Aftermath

Elena stood in the clearing, her body trembling. The warmth of the deer's blood still lingered on her lips, the taste of it burned into her mind. She stared at the lifeless animal in disbelief, the full weight of what she had done pressing down on her chest.

She had killed.

The thought made her stomach turn, and she stumbled backward, her mind racing. How had she lost control so easily? It had been instinctual—no thought, just action. One moment, she was running through the woods, desperate to escape the hunger; the next, she was feeding off the blood of a helpless creature.

She had become a predator.

Her father's journal had warned her about this—the early stages of transformation, the overwhelming urge to feed. She could remember reading the passages about his own struggles, how he had fought the cravings for months before he finally succumbed.

And now, here she was, standing on the same precipice.

"No," she whispered to herself. "I won't become like him. I won't."

But the hunger had been so powerful. It had almost consumed her. And now, after feeding, there was a part of her that felt... stronger. More alive. It frightened her how much she had enjoyed it, the rush of power that surged through her as she drank.

Shaking her head, Elena forced herself to move. She needed to get back to the house. She couldn't stay out here, not like this. Her legs felt weak as she stumbled through the forest, her mind clouded with the memory of the blood.

As she approached the manor, the familiar sight of its gothic spires rising above the trees filled her with a strange sense of dread. The house had always been a place of darkness, but now it felt even more oppressive, like it was closing in on her.

Once inside, she collapsed onto the floor of the foyer, her breath coming in ragged gasps. Her hands were still stained with blood, and she stared at them in horror. What was happening to her?

Her thoughts spiraled as the reality of her situation sank in. She had fed on an animal tonight, but what if next time… it wasn't an animal? What if the hunger grew stronger? What if she couldn't stop herself?

The memory of her father's journal echoed in her mind. The curse of the Sinclair family—the curse of the vampire. It wasn't just a myth, and now it was happening to her. She needed to find a way to stop it before it was too late.

But the more she thought about it, the more a new, terrifying thought began to creep into her mind. What if she didn't want to stop it?

What if part of her wanted this power?

Chapter 6: Dark Temptations

The days that followed were a blur of conflicting emotions. Elena isolated herself in the manor, haunted by the growing hunger and the memory of that night in the woods. The more she tried to push the thoughts away, the more they clawed at the edges of her mind.

She spent hours pouring over her father's journals, searching for answers, but they offered little comfort. Nathaniel Sinclair had been a brilliant man, but his research was incomplete, and his descent into madness was well documented in the pages. He had tried to resist the curse, but in the end, it had consumed him.

Elena knew she had to fight, but the battle was harder than she anticipated. Every day, the hunger grew stronger. She could feel it gnawing at her insides, a constant, unrelenting pressure. The world around her became sharper, her senses heightened in ways she didn't fully understand. The scent of the earth, the distant heartbeat of creatures in the forest, the sound of her own blood rushing through her veins—it was all overwhelming.

She tried to keep herself busy, exploring the old manor, reading books, trying to distract herself from the growing urge to feed. But it was no use. The hunger was always there, lurking just beneath the surface.

It wasn't until the third night that she realized something was wrong.

She woke up in the middle of the night, drenched in sweat, her body aching with a strange heat. The hunger was stronger than ever, more insistent, like a living thing inside her. She could feel her pulse racing, her skin tingling with an unfamiliar sensation.

Without thinking, she found herself drawn to the window. The moon was full, casting a pale light over the grounds of the estate. She could hear the faint sounds of the night—the rustle of leaves, the distant call of an owl, the soft shuffle of something moving through the trees.

And then she heard it—the sound that sent a jolt of energy through her body.

A heartbeat.

But this time, it wasn't an animal. It was human.

Elena's breath caught in her throat as she pressed her hand against the cold glass of the window. The sound was faint, but unmistakable. Someone was nearby, walking through the woods.

Her mind screamed at her to turn away, to lock herself in her room and fight the urge. But her body was already moving, her feet carrying her out of the bedroom and down the stairs before she even realized what she was doing.

The front door creaked as she opened it, the cool night air washing over her as she stepped outside. Her senses were on high alert, every sound amplified, every scent sharper than before. She could hear the faint crunch of footsteps on the forest floor, growing closer.

A figure emerged from the trees—a man, maybe in his mid-thirties, dressed in a coat and hat, carrying a flashlight. He was walking slowly, cautiously, as though searching for something.

Elena's mouth went dry. She could hear his heartbeat now, loud and rhythmic, calling to her in a way that was impossible to ignore.

She clenched her fists, digging her nails into her palms in an attempt to ground herself. "Don't do this," she whispered to herself. "Don't let it control you."

But the hunger was too strong. She could feel her control slipping away, just like it had that night with the deer. The man's heartbeat was like a siren's call, pulling her closer with every passing second.

She took a step forward, then another, her eyes locked on him. The world around her faded, and all she could hear was the sound of his pulse, the rush of blood through his veins.

"Excuse me," the man called, his voice breaking through her haze. He hadn't seen her yet, but his flashlight swept in her direction, the beam of light cutting through the darkness. "I'm lost. Do you know—?"

His words were cut off as his eyes met hers.

Elena froze, her breath catching in her throat. The hunger roared inside her, demanding that she act, that she take what she needed. But something in the man's gaze stopped her—something familiar.

"Lucas?" she whispered.

The man lowered the flashlight, his brow furrowing in confusion. "Elena? Is that you?"

It was Lucas—her childhood friend, the detective she hadn't seen in years. His voice, his presence, snapped her back to reality. The hunger was still there, burning inside her, but she managed to pull back, to regain control.

"What are you doing here?" she asked, her voice shaky.

"I came to check on you," Lucas replied, taking a step closer. "You weren't answering your phone, and I was worried. What's going on? Why are you out here in the middle of the night?"

Elena's mind raced. She had to think quickly, had to find a way to explain why she was standing alone in the woods, half-crazed and on the verge of losing control. "I... I couldn't sleep," she said, avoiding his gaze. "I needed some air."

Lucas didn't look convinced. He took another step toward her, his eyes scanning her face, searching for answers. "Are you okay? You look... different."

"I'm fine," Elena said quickly, backing away from him. The last thing she needed was for Lucas to get too close. She could still hear the steady beat of his heart, still feel the hunger gnawing at her insides. If he got any closer, she wasn't sure she could stop herself.

"I don't believe you," Lucas said, his voice firm. "Something's wrong, Elena. I know you better than that."

She felt a surge of panic. He was right—he knew her too well. He could see through her lies, could sense that something was terribly wrong. But how could she explain it? How could she tell him that she was turning into a monster?

"I just need some time," she said, trying to keep her voice steady. "Please, Lucas. Just go."

But he didn't move. He stood there, watching her, his face full of concern. "I'm not leaving you out here alone," he said softly. "Whatever's going on, we'll figure it out together."

Elena's resolve crumbled. She wanted to tell him everything, to let him in, to ask for his help. But the hunger was too strong. She couldn't trust herself—not with him.

Before she could respond, Lucas reached out, placing a hand on her shoulder. The warmth of his touch sent a shockwave through her body, and she recoiled, stepping back sharply.

"Don't!" she shouted, her voice sharper than she intended.

Lucas's hand dropped; his face clouded with confusion. "Elena… what's happening to you?"

Tears welled in her eyes. She wanted to tell him the truth, but she couldn't. Not now. Not like this.

"Please," she whispered, her voice breaking. "Just go."

Lucas hesitated for a long moment, his gaze lingering on her face. Then, finally, he nodded. "Okay," he said softly. "But I'm not giving up on you."

He turned and disappeared back into the woods, leaving Elena standing alone in the darkness, her heart pounding in her chest.

As soon as he was gone, the hunger came rushing back, fiercer than ever. She sank to the ground, her body shaking with the effort of resisting it.

The temptation was overwhelming.

And she wasn't sure how much longer she could fight it.

Chapter 7: Fractured

Elena watched the shadows swallow Lucas as he disappeared into the forest. Her legs gave out, and she collapsed to the ground, her body trembling with the effort to hold herself together. The hunger, the need for blood, was a constant ache now, a pressure that threatened to tear her apart.

How close she had come to losing control. If Lucas hadn't recognized her, hadn't pulled her back from the brink... she didn't even want to think about what might have happened. The image of him, pale and drained, his body lifeless at her feet, flashed through her mind, and a sob broke from her chest.

She couldn't stay here any longer.

The manor, the curse—it was all too much. She needed to leave before she hurt someone, before the hunger took her over completely. But as she stood and made her way back to the house, something stopped her. A voice, deep inside, that whispered against her panic.

Running won't help you.

She froze, the echo of the voice reverberating through her mind. It wasn't her voice, and yet it was. It was darker, more primal, filled with a strange sort of power.

You can't outrun what's inside of you, the voice whispered again.

Elena shook her head, trying to banish the thought, but it clung to her like a shadow. The hunger, the curse—it wasn't something she could simply leave behind. It was part of her now, woven into the very fabric of her being. No matter how far she ran, it would follow her.

There's only one way to stop this, the voice continued, softer now, more coaxing. *You need to understand it. Embrace it.*

"No," Elena whispered to herself, her voice shaky. "I won't."

You can't fight forever.

She stumbled back into the manor, the heavy front door creaking shut behind her. Her mind was a swirl of confusion and fear. How much longer could she fight the hunger? How much longer could she hold on to her humanity?

Her thoughts went to her father's journal, the pages filled with his frantic attempts to stop the transformation. He had fought the curse, just as she was doing, but in the end, it had consumed him. The pages had stopped abruptly, no mention of what had finally happened to him, but Elena knew.

Her father had become a vampire.

Chapter 8 The Hunger

She collapsed onto the old couch in the sitting room, her body heavy with exhaustion. The hunger ebbed slightly now that she was back inside, but it still gnawed at her, a constant reminder of the battle she was waging. She had been foolish to think she could simply walk away from this. The curse wasn't something she could escape.

Maybe Lennox was right, she thought. Maybe the answer wasn't in running, but in understanding what was happening to her. Her father's journals, the research, it was all a part of that. But there was one thing Lennox had warned her about that she couldn't shake from her mind—the Elder Vampire.

If there was anyone who knew the truth, who understood the full extent of the curse, it was him.

But to seek him out was dangerous. Dr. Lennox had made that clear. The Elder Vampire was powerful, ancient, and far beyond the control of any mortal.

But what choice do I have?

Elena sat up, staring at the fireplace, the flames dancing in front of her eyes. She couldn't stay here forever, waiting for the hunger to take over. She had to take control of her own fate, and if that meant seeking out the very creature responsible for her family's curse, so be it.

She would face the Elder Vampire. She would find a way to stop this, or at the very least, understand it.

Chapter 9: The First Step

The next morning, Elena packed a small bag and prepared herself for the journey. The decision to leave Sinclair Manor felt surreal. For so long, she had been trapped here, both physically and emotionally, by the weight of her family's legacy. Now, she was about to leave it behind, possibly forever.

She had no idea where to begin her search for the Elder Vampire. Her father's journals offered some clues, vague mentions of ancient covens and secret locations, but nothing concrete. Still, it was better than nothing. She would start with the closest town and go from there.

Lucas's face flashed through her mind, a knot tightening in her chest. She didn't know how she would explain her sudden disappearance to him—or if she should explain it at all. The less he knew, the safer he would be.

The thought of seeing him again after nearly losing control filled her with dread. He was already suspicious, his detective instincts clearly telling him that something was wrong. If she stayed any longer, he would figure out the truth, and she couldn't allow that.

The front door groaned as she pushed it open, the crisp morning air greeting her. She turned back one last time, her eyes sweeping over the grand, decaying estate that had been her family's home for generations. It felt strange, like she was walking away from something important, but at the same time, leaving behind a prison.

The road leading away from the manor was long and winding, but as she began walking, a sense of resolve filled her. She didn't know what she would find, or if she would even survive the encounter with the Elder Vampire, but she couldn't let fear stop her.

Hours passed as she made her way toward the town. The trees closed in on either side of her, their branches swaying in the light breeze. Every now and then, a noise from the forest—a rustle of leaves, the snap of a twig—made her tense, her heightened senses always on alert.

The hunger still simmered beneath the surface, but it was manageable for now. She hadn't fed since the night of the deer, and while the cravings were growing stronger, she could still control them. Barely.

As the town came into view, Elena felt a strange sense of disconnection. It had been so long since she had been around people, she wasn't sure how to act anymore. She kept her head down as she walked through the streets, avoiding eye contact with the few locals she passed. Her senses were overloaded by the sounds and smells of the town—the faint aroma of cooking food, the sound of distant conversation, the steady thrum of human life.

It was too much.

Elena made her way to the nearest inn and booked a room. It was small and unremarkable, but it would give her a place to gather her thoughts and plan her next move. She needed to find information, old legends, or any rumors that could lead her to the Elder Vampire.

But first, she needed to control the hunger.

Chapter 10: The Hunger Returns

Elena stared at herself in the cracked mirror of the inn's bathroom. Her reflection was pale, her eyes shadowed with exhaustion. The hunger was back with a vengeance, stronger now that she was surrounded by people. She could hear the sounds of life just beyond the thin walls—the faint heartbeat of the innkeeper downstairs, the soft breathing of someone in the room next door. It was a constant temptation, and she could feel herself slipping, the tight control she had been holding onto for so long starting to unravel.

Her hands gripped the edge of the sink, knuckles white. "Not now," she whispered to herself. "Not here."

She needed to feed, but she couldn't risk drawing attention to herself, not in a town where every stranger was noticed. But the thought of leaving the town, wandering into the woods to find another animal, filled her with a deep sense of dread. It wouldn't be enough. She knew it wouldn't.

The hunger demanded more.

Her mind raced, searching for a solution. If she didn't feed soon, she would lose control. The memories of that night with the deer flooded back—how easily she had given in, how intoxicating it had felt. The thought of doing the same to a human terrified her, but at the same time, the hunger whispered that it was inevitable.

There was a knock on the door, and Elena flinched, her body going rigid.

"Miss Sinclair?" came the innkeeper's voice from the other side. "Just wanted to let you know we've got supper ready downstairs if you're hungry."

Elena clenched her fists, the irony of his words hitting her like a punch to the gut. Hungry. That didn't even begin to describe what she was feeling.

"I'm not hungry," she called back, her voice tight.

There was a brief pause, then the innkeeper's footsteps retreated down the hall.

Elena exhaled slowly, her body shaking with the effort of control. She couldn't stay here much longer. The temptation was too great, the risk too high. If she gave in, if she fed on a human, she wasn't sure she would ever be able to forgive herself.

With a sudden resolve, she grabbed her bag and threw it over her shoulder. She needed to get out of town, away from people, before it was too late.

As she stepped outside into the cool night air, the hunger gnawed at her like a wild animal. She was running out of time.

Chapter 11: Into the Night

The night was darker than usual, the moon hidden behind thick clouds that obscured the sky. Elena walked briskly down the empty streets of the town, her senses on edge. Every sound, every faint heartbeat from the buildings she passed, felt like a taunt—a reminder of the hunger that clawed at her insides.

She needed to get away, to find somewhere secluded where she could think clearly. The woods surrounding the town stretched for miles, and that's where she headed, the trees calling to her like a refuge from the chaos inside her mind.

As she moved deeper into the forest, the sounds of civilization faded, replaced by the rustling of leaves and the distant calls of nocturnal animals. It was quiet here, the air cool and crisp. But even in the stillness of the woods, the hunger followed her.

She could hear it now—the faint, steady pulse of life in the distance. Not human this time, but animal. She could smell it too, the scent of fur and warm blood. Her body responded instinctively, her heart racing, her feet carrying her toward the source.

It was another deer, grazing quietly in a small clearing, unaware of her presence.

Elena stopped at the edge of the clearing, her breath coming in short, sharp gasps. The hunger roared inside her, screaming at her to act, to feed. But something in her resisted. The memory of Lucas, the sound of his heartbeat as he stood before her, flashed through her mind.

She wasn't a monster. Not yet.

With a deep breath, Elena closed her eyes and willed herself to turn away from the deer. She could fight this. She had to.

But before she could move, a sound from behind her froze her in place.

Footsteps.

Slow, deliberate, moving toward her through the trees.

Elena spun around, her body tense, her senses on high alert. Her eyes scanned the shadows, but she saw nothing. The footsteps stopped.

"Who's there?" she called, her voice trembling slightly.

There was no response, but the air around her seemed to grow colder, the hairs on the back of her neck standing on end. She took a cautious step forward, her heart pounding in her chest.

And then she heard it—a voice, low and smooth, filled with a chilling sort of calm.

"You're looking for me, aren't you?"

Elena's blood ran cold. The voice came from the shadows, but she couldn't see its source.

"I know who you are," the voice continued. "You've come for answers."

A figure stepped out of the darkness, his movements unnaturally smooth and graceful. He was tall, dressed in dark clothing that blended seamlessly with the night, his pale skin almost glowing in the faint moonlight. His eyes, a deep, unnatural red, locked onto hers with a predatory intensity.

Elena's breath caught in her throat.

The Elder Vampire.

Chapter 12: The Encounter

Elena stood frozen as the figure of the Elder Vampire emerged from the shadows. His presence radiated an ancient power, his movements fluid and purposeful. Everything about him screamed danger, yet Elena couldn't tear her eyes away. Her breath caught in her throat, her heart pounding as a mixture of fear and curiosity overtook her.

"Who… who are you?" she asked, though she already knew the answer.

The Elder Vampire's lips curved into a slow, almost amused smile. "You know who I am, Elena Sinclair. I've been watching you."

The sound of his voice sent a shiver down her spine. It was deep and smooth, with a strange, hypnotic quality. Elena took a cautious step back, her instincts screaming at her to run, but the hunger inside her flared at the sight of him. It was as if her own blood recognized him, drawn to the immense power he exuded.

"You've come seeking answers," he continued, his voice calm, as though he had all the time in the world. "Answers about the curse. About who you are."

Elena swallowed hard, trying to gather her thoughts. She had come looking for him, that much was true, but standing here in his presence, she realized just how unprepared she was. The weight of his gaze made her feel exposed, vulnerable, as if he could see into the deepest parts of her soul.

"I want to know how to stop this," she said, her voice steadier than she felt. "The curse… it's destroying me."

The Elder Vampire took a slow step forward, his movements eerily graceful. "Destroying you? Or awakening you?"

Elena frowned, confused by his words. "Awakening?"

He stopped a few feet away from her, his eyes locking onto hers with an intensity that made her skin prickle. "You feel it, don't you? The power within you, growing stronger every day. You can hear the heartbeat of those around you, smell the scent of their blood. It frightens you, but it also tempts you."

Elena's breath hitched. He was right. The power that came with the curse was terrifying, but there was a part of her—no matter how small—that was drawn to it. The heightened senses, the strength, the rush of control. But the fear of losing herself, of becoming a monster, outweighed it.

"I don't want this," she said, her voice barely a whisper. "I don't want to become a monster."

The Elder Vampire's smile faded, his expression growing serious. "A monster? Is that what you think I am?"

Elena's heart raced. She had heard the stories, had read about the carnage and destruction vampires could cause, the lives they consumed. But standing here in front of the Elder Vampire, she felt something more complicated. Yes, he was dangerous, and yes, he was ancient and powerful, but there was something more—something deeper, almost tragic, in his eyes.

"I don't know what you are," she admitted, her voice shaking. "But I don't want to lose myself."

The Elder Vampire's gaze softened, but there was still a flicker of amusement in his eyes. "Lose yourself? You misunderstand the nature of the curse. It's not about losing who you are. It's about discovering what you truly are."

Elena shook her head, confused. "I don't want to be like you."

He tilted his head slightly, studying her. "You think you have a choice? This curse is not something you can simply cast aside. It is in your blood, in your very soul. Fighting it will only make the transformation more painful."

Elena clenched her fists, anger flaring within her. "So what? I'm supposed to just give in? Let the vampire take over and forget who I am?"

The Elder Vampire's expression darkened. "No. But you must learn to control it. The hunger, the power—they are part of you now, whether you like it or not. If you do not master it, it will master you."

His words struck something deep inside her, something she had been avoiding since the moment she realized the curse was real. She had been so focused on resisting, on trying to stop the transformation, that she hadn't considered what it would mean to truly accept it—to control it rather than be controlled by it.

"I can't," she said, her voice faltering. "I don't know how."

The Elder Vampire took another step closer, his gaze softening. "I can teach you."

Elena's heart skipped a beat. His offer was tempting, but it was also dangerous. Accepting his help meant stepping deeper into the world of darkness, and she wasn't sure if she could ever come back from that. But what choice did she have? If she didn't learn to control the hunger, it would consume her.

"What do you want in return?" she asked, her voice wary.

The Elder Vampire smiled, a slow, predatory grin. "Nothing. You are already bound to me by blood. What happens to you happens to me."

Elena frowned. "Bound to you? What does that mean?"

His eyes glinted in the moonlight. "The curse that runs through your veins is ancient, passed down from my own bloodline. I am the one who first gave it to your ancestor, Lucius Sinclair, centuries ago. You and I are connected, Elena, whether you realize it or not."

Her stomach churned at the revelation. The curse wasn't just a random affliction—it was tied directly to him, to the creature standing before her. She was part of his legacy, part of a chain that stretched back through generations.

"I don't want this connection," she said, her voice trembling with defiance.

The Elder Vampire's smile faded, his expression hardening. "It is not for you to want or reject. It is simply what is. But you must decide now—will you continue to fight what you are, or will you let me show you how to control it?"

Elena's mind raced. If she refused him, she would be left to face the curse on her own, with no guidance, no control. But accepting his offer meant trusting him, a creature who had lived for centuries and who had cursed her family in the first place.

Chapter 13: A Dangerous Choice

Elena returned to the inn that night, her mind heavy with the weight of what had just happened. The Elder Vampire's offer haunted her thoughts. He had presented her with a choice—learn to control the curse, or be consumed by it. But trusting him felt like stepping into a trap.

As she paced the small room, she tried to weigh her options. If she rejected his help, what hope did she have of mastering the curse on her own? Dr. Lennox's warnings echoed in her mind. He had made it clear that the Elder Vampire was dangerous, that seeking him out would only lead to disaster. But Lennox hadn't experienced the hunger. He didn't know what it was like to feel it tearing at her insides, demanding to be fed.

And Lucas—what would Lucas think if he knew what she was becoming? She had already come so close to losing control around him. What would happen if she stayed in his life? How long before she hurt him, or worse?

Her hands trembled as she sank onto the bed, her head in her hands. She had never felt so alone, so trapped by the impossible choices in front of her.

There was a soft knock at the door, and Elena stiffened, her heart racing. For a moment, she thought it might be Lucas, coming to check on her again. But when she opened the door, it was the innkeeper, holding a small tray of food.

"Miss, I noticed you haven't eaten," he said kindly, his warm eyes full of concern. "I thought I'd bring you something."

Elena's throat tightened. The smell of the food was overwhelming, but it wasn't the meal that tempted her. It was the innkeeper himself—the steady beat of his heart, the warmth radiating from his body. The hunger roared to life, and she had to grip the edge of the door to steady herself.

"I—thank you," she stammered, her voice hoarse. "But I'm not hungry."

The innkeeper frowned, clearly confused, but he nodded and set the tray down just inside the door. "If you need anything, just let me know."

Elena forced a tight smile and shut the door, leaning against it as she fought to control the hunger. It was getting worse, harder to resist with each passing hour.

She couldn't do this. Not alone.

Her mind returned to the Elder Vampire's offer. He had said they were bound by blood, that he could help her control the curse. As much as she feared him, as much as she wanted to believe she could resist, deep down, she knew the truth.

She needed him.

Chapter 14: Into the Darkness

The next night, Elena found herself standing at the edge

 of the forest, waiting. The wind rustled through the trees, carrying with it the sounds of the night—the distant call of an owl, the soft rustle of leaves. She knew he would come. He had been watching her, and he would know that she had made her decision.

Her heart pounded in her chest as she waited, her eyes scanning the shadows. Part of her still screamed at her to run, to leave this place and never look back. But another part, the part that was growing stronger with each passing day, urged her forward.

And then, as if summoned by her thoughts, he appeared.

The Elder Vampire stepped out of the darkness; his movements as graceful as before. His red eyes gleamed in the moonlight, and his lips curved into that familiar, knowing smile.

"You've made your choice," he said, his voice low and smooth.

Elena swallowed hard and nodded. "Yes."

He stepped closer, his gaze never leaving hers. "Good. Then we begin."

Chapter 15: The First Lesson

The air between them was electric as the Elder Vampire stepped closer, his presence commanding and undeniable. Elena's pulse raced, her mind buzzing with a mix of fear and curiosity. She had made her choice, and now there was no turning back.

He studied her for a moment, as if assessing her readiness. "The first lesson," he began, his voice quiet but firm, "is understanding the hunger. It's not your enemy, Elena. It's a part of you, just as vital as the blood in your veins."

She flinched at his words, instinctively recoiling. "It's not a part of me. It's a curse."

The Elder Vampire's lips twitched into a faint smile. "A curse? Perhaps. But curses often bring power. It's only a curse because you fear it, because you resist it. When you stop fighting, when you embrace the hunger, you will find strength beyond anything you've ever known."

Elena clenched her fists, her body tense. "I don't want to be a killer."

He stepped even closer, his gaze penetrating. "Then don't kill. Feed without destruction.

There is a balance, but you must learn to control the hunger before it controls you."

She shook her head, struggling to grasp what he was telling her. "How? How do I control something that feels so… overwhelming?"

The Elder Vampire extended his hand, palm up. "Trust me, and I will show you."

Hesitantly, Elena reached out and took his hand, her fingers trembling as they brushed against his cold skin. His touch was like ice, sending a shiver down her spine, but there was a strange comfort in it as well—a connection that felt undeniable.

"Close your eyes," he instructed, his voice low and soothing.

Elena obeyed, her heart racing as she stood there, her hand in his, the night closing in around them.

"Focus on the hunger," he whispered. "Feel it in your body, your blood. Don't fight it—let it rise."

Her body stiffened as the hunger surged to the surface, roaring inside her like a caged beast. Every instinct told her to resist, to shove it down, but the Elder Vampire's words echoed in her mind. *Don't fight it.*

Elena took a deep breath and allowed the hunger to rise, allowed herself to feel it fully. It was terrifying, powerful, and primal, but as she let it flow through her, something shifted. The hunger no longer felt like a wild, uncontrollable force. It was still strong, still dangerous, but it was also something she could shape, something she could command.

"That's it," the Elder Vampire said softly, his voice encouraging. "Now, open your eyes."

When Elena opened her eyes, the world around her had changed. Everything was sharper, more vivid. She could see the veins of every leaf in the trees, the minute details of the bark, the subtle movements of the insects hidden in the grass. The scent of the night air filled her lungs, rich with life and the promise of blood.

"You see?" the Elder Vampire asked, his eyes gleaming. "This is what it means to embrace the hunger."

Elena's breath caught in her throat. She could feel it—the power coursing through her body, heightening her senses, making her stronger. But it wasn't just the power. It was the control. She could feel the hunger, but it no longer dominated her. She was no longer a slave to it.

"It... different," she murmured, her voice barely above a whisper.

The Elder Vampire released her hand and stepped back, his smile widening. "You're learning."

But even as the power surged through her, there was a part of Elena that recoiled. Was this really what she wanted? To give in to the hunger, to become something more than human? The thought both excited and terrified her.

"How do I stop it from taking over completely?" she asked, her voice wavering.

The Elder Vampire's smile faded slightly, and his expression grew serious. "That is the second lesson. Power must be balanced with control. The more you feed, the stronger you become, but the risk of losing yourself increases."

Elena's heart sank. "So, it's inevitable? If I use this power, I'll eventually lose who I am?"

"Not if you are careful," he replied. "You must set boundaries, rules for yourself. You must decide who you are and what you are willing to become. But remember, Elena, power always comes with a price. You cannot have one without the other."

His words hung in the air between them, heavy with meaning. She understood now what he was offering—not just control over the curse, but a chance to wield the power it brought. But at what cost?

"What do you want from me?" she asked suddenly, the question burning in her mind. "Why help me?"

The Elder Vampire regarded her for a long moment before speaking. "As I said before, we are bound by blood. What affects you, affects me. But there is more." He paused, his eyes narrowing slightly. "I have lived many lifetimes, Elena. I have seen civilizations rise and fall, watched countless people come and go. But you… you are different."

Elena frowned. "Different how?"

He stepped closer, his gaze intense. "You are the last of your bloodline, the final link to the curse I bestowed upon your ancestor. Your survival is important, not just to you, but to me. You are part of something far greater than yourself, and together, we can shape what comes next."

Elena's chest tightened. His words stirred something deep inside her—something that felt like destiny, like a path she had been walking long before she even knew it existed. But at the same time, it filled her with a sense of foreboding.

"What if I don't want to be part of this?" she asked, her voice barely above a whisper. "What if I just want to live a normal life?"

The Elder Vampire's expression softened, but there was a sadness in his eyes. "There is no normal life for us, Elena. Not anymore."

The weight of his words sank into her, and for the first time, she truly understood the gravity of the situation. There was no going back. She was no longer the person she had been before the hunger began to change her. That life—her life—was over.

"What happens now?" she asked, her voice hollow.

The Elder Vampire's smile returned, but it was tinged with something darker. "Now, we continue your training. There is much you need to learn if you are to survive."

Elena nodded, though her heart was heavy. She had made her choice, but the path ahead was more uncertain than ever. She didn't fully trust the Elder Vampire, but she couldn't deny that she needed him. She had seen what the hunger could do—how easily it could take over—and she knew that without his help, she would lose herself completely.

But as they began to walk deeper into the forest, side by side, Elena couldn't shake the feeling that she was walking into a trap— one that had been set long before she was even born.

Chapter 15: Blood and Secrets

The following weeks blurred into a strange routine of training and secrecy. Every night, Elena met the Elder Vampire in the woods, and every night, he pushed her to confront the power within her. He taught her how to control the hunger, how to feed without killing, and how to use her heightened senses to her advantage.

But with every lesson, the lines between right and wrong grew blurrier.

Elena learned to feed on animals, to draw only enough blood to satisfy the hunger without causing harm. But the more she fed, the more she craved something stronger, something richer. The blood of animals dulled the hunger, but it didn't quench it. It was a pale imitation of what her body truly desired.

Human blood.

The thought of it repulsed her, but the temptation grew stronger with each passing day. The Elder Vampire never encouraged her to feed on humans, but he didn't discourage it either. He simply reminded her that power came with a price, and that it was up to her to decide how far she was willing to go.

In the daylight hours, Elena stayed in the town, hiding her growing transformation from the people around her. She saw Lucas only in passing, avoiding his questions and his worried glances. She knew he was suspicious, but she couldn't risk telling him the truth—not yet. Not until she had a better handle on the curse.

But Lucas wasn't the only one watching her. She could feel eyes on her whenever she walked through the streets, a sense of being followed. At first, she thought it was paranoia, but soon she realized that something—someone—was keeping tabs on her.

One evening, as she made her way back to the woods for another lesson, she heard it: the unmistakable sound of footsteps trailing her, trying to stay hidden but not quite succeeding.

Elena's heart raced. She quickened her pace, darting into a narrow alleyway between two buildings. The footsteps followed, growing closer.

Without thinking, she whirled around, her heightened senses kicking in. She caught a glimpse of a figure, cloaked in shadow, moving toward her.

"Who are you?" she demanded, her voice cold and sharp.

The figure hesitated for a moment, then stepped into the dim light of a streetlamp. It was a woman, tall and lean, her face partially obscured by a hood. Her eyes glinted in the darkness, but they weren't like the Elder Vampire's—they were human.

"Elena Sinclair," the woman said, her voice low and smooth. "You're in danger."

Elena's pulse quickened. "Who are you?"

The woman smiled faintly, but there was no warmth in it. "Someone who knows what you're becoming. Someone who wants to help."

Elena took a cautious step back, her instincts screaming at her to be wary. "Why should I trust you?"

The woman's expression darkened. "Because if you don't, the Elder Vampire will destroy you."

Elena's blood ran cold. "What are you talking about?"

"You think he's helping you," the woman said, her voice edged with warning. "But you're just a pawn in his game. He's been planning this for centuries. And you, Elena, are the final piece."

The words hit Elena like a punch to the gut. Everything she had been feeling—the doubt, the fear, the sense of being manipulated—it all came crashing down. But she couldn't let herself believe it. Not yet.

"Why should I believe anything you say?" Elena asked, her voice shaking.

The woman took a step closer, her eyes gleaming with intensity. "Because I know the truth about the curse. And I know how to break it."

Chapter 16: The Truth in Shadows

Elena stood frozen, her heart pounding in her chest. The woman's words echoed in her mind, each one more unsettling than the last.

The Elder Vampire had warned her about many things, but never had he hinted at being a danger to her. And yet, here this stranger stood, claiming he had been manipulating her all along.

"What do you mean, he's been planning this for centuries?" Elena asked, her voice laced with suspicion. "And how do you know so much about the curse?"

The woman pulled back her hood, revealing dark hair streaked with gray and piercing, weathered eyes that seemed to carry the weight of years of knowledge. Her face was sharp, lined with age, but her posture remained strong, as though she had been through a thousand battles and was ready for one more.

"My name is Isolde," the woman said, her voice softer now but still filled with a cold determination. "I've been watching the Sinclair bloodline for centuries. I've seen what the Elder Vampire has done to your family, and I've seen how it ends. You're not the first, Elena, and you won't be the last—unless you stop him."

Elena took a step back, her mind racing. "Watching my family? Why?"

Isolde's expression darkened, her eyes narrowing. "Because long ago, I was like you. I, too, was cursed. But I found a way to resist, to escape his grasp before I could become fully like him. And I've been trying to stop him ever since."

Elena's stomach churned. The idea that this stranger had once been in her shoes, that she had faced the same curse and survived, was both comforting and terrifying. But at the same time, the idea that the Elder Vampire had orchestrated everything, manipulating her family for centuries, seemed too incredible to believe.

"You're telling me that the Elder Vampire has been cursing my family on purpose? Why would he do that?" Elena asked, her voice rising with frustration. "Why keep us alive at all?"

"Because he needs you," Isolde replied, stepping closer. "The curse binds him to your bloodline. He's been trapped, limited in his power, and every generation, he comes closer to breaking free. You, Elena, are the last key. If he completes the ritual, he will finally break the bond that holds him, and he will be unstoppable."

Elena's heart hammered in her chest. "What ritual?"

Isolde's eyes flickered with urgency. "He didn't tell you? Of course not. The Elder Vampire has always been careful. The ritual requires the last living descendant of the Sinclair family—your blood, Elena. He's been grooming you, making you stronger, teaching you to control the hunger, all to prepare you for that moment."

"No," Elena whispered, shaking her head. "That can't be true. He—he's been helping me. Teaching me how to control it, how to survive."

Isolde's lips twisted into a bitter smile. "He's been teaching you how to *serve* him. Every lesson, every step of the way, he's been preparing you to be the final piece in his plan."

Elena staggered backward, her mind reeling. She didn't want to believe it. The Elder Vampire had been her guide, the one who had shown her how to navigate the terrifying transformation she was undergoing. But could it really have been a lie? Could he have been using her all along?

"There's more," Isolde continued, her voice soft but insistent. "The bond between you and him—it's more than just the curse. If he succeeds, you'll lose everything. Your humanity, your soul. You'll become a vessel for his power."

Elena's breath hitched, the gravity of Isolde's words sinking in. "How do I stop it? How do I stop him?"

Isolde's face hardened. "The ritual hasn't been completed yet, which means there's still time. You need to cut the bond before he can use you. The curse is tied to his blood, just as it is to yours. If you sever the connection, you free yourself—and you weaken him."

"But how?" Elena asked, desperation creeping into her voice. "How do I break the bond?"

Isolde hesitated, her eyes searching Elena's face. "There's a ritual, a counter-ritual, hidden in the oldest records of your family.

It was passed down through your bloodline as a way to protect against the curse, but it's been lost over time. Your father… he was searching for it."

"My father?" Elena's voice cracked at the mention of him. "He was trying to break the curse?"

Isolde nodded. "He found fragments of the ritual, but he didn't have time to complete it. That's why the Elder Vampire let him live for so long—because your father was close. And now, you need to finish what he started."

Elena's mind whirled. Her father had been fighting against the curse all along, but she had thought he'd succumbed to it. Now, everything felt more complex, more dangerous than she had ever imagined.

"How do I find this ritual?" Elena asked, her voice trembling with urgency.

"You need to go back," Isolde said quietly. "Back to Sinclair Manor. Your father's research is still there. It's hidden in the places where only a Sinclair would think to look."

Elena's breath caught. Returning to the manor—the thought alone filled her with dread. But she knew she didn't have a choice. If what Isolde said was true, then the answers she needed were hidden in the house where her father had fought and lost his final battle against the curse.

"I'll go," Elena said, determination hardening in her voice. "I'll find the ritual and break the bond."

Isolde nodded, but her eyes remained serious. "You must be careful. The Elder Vampire won't let you go easily. He knows you're close to figuring out the truth. He'll do anything to stop you."

Elena's chest tightened. "What about you? Will you help me?"

Isolde's gaze softened, but there was a flicker of something dark in her eyes. "I can't go with you, Elena. The Elder Vampire has his hold on me too. I've fought him for centuries, but if I get too close, he'll know, and he'll stop us both."

Elena swallowed hard, her mind racing. She was on her own in this, just as she had been since the day she learned about the curse. But this time, she had a plan. She had hope, however fragile it was.

"Then I'll go alone," Elena said, squaring her shoulders. "I'll finish what my father started."

Isolde stepped forward and placed a hand on Elena's shoulder, her grip firm. "You're stronger than you think, Elena. The power inside you—it's a double-edged sword. Use it wisely, and it can be your greatest weapon."

Elena nodded, though doubt still gnawed at her insides. She had been trained by the Elder Vampire, and now she had to use everything he had taught her to stop him. The irony wasn't lost on her, but there was no time for regret. She had to act quickly, before the hunger consumed her and before the Elder Vampire could complete his plan.

As she turned to leave, Isolde called out one final warning. "Elena, be careful who you trust. The Elder Vampire isn't the only one with an agenda. There are others who would use you for their own ends."

Elena paused, glancing over her shoulder. "What do you mean?"

Isolde's eyes darkened. "The world of vampires is full of lies and power struggles.

Everyone has a role to play, and not all of them are as clear as they seem."

With that cryptic warning hanging in the air, Elena left the alley and slipped back into the shadows. The streets of the town were quiet, but she could feel the weight of eyes watching her from the darkness. She was a pawn in a game she didn't fully understand, but one thing was certain—she had to get to Sinclair Manor, and she had to do it fast.

Chapter 16: Return to the Manor

The journey back to Sinclair Manor was a blur. Elena's thoughts churned as she retraced the familiar path, the weight of her decision pressing down on her with each step. The old, decaying house loomed in the distance, its spires barely visible against the darkening sky. This place had always felt like a prison, but now it was her only hope.

As she reached the front gates, a wave of memories flooded her. The house had been abandoned for years, and yet it felt alive with secrets, as if the walls themselves were waiting for her to uncover the truth.

Elena pushed open the rusted gate and made her way up the cracked stone steps. The air was thick with tension, the quiet unnerving. She stepped inside, the door creaking loudly, and the familiar scent of damp wood and decay filled her lungs.

The darkness inside the manor swallowed her, but Elena moved with purpose. She knew where she needed to go—her father's study. It was the heart of the house, the place where her father had spent endless hours researching the curse that had plagued their family. If there were answers, they would be there.

As she made her way through the narrow hallways, the sound of her footsteps echoed in the silence. The memories of her childhood haunted every corner, but she couldn't let herself dwell on them now. There was too much at stake.

When she finally reached the study, Elena hesitated. The door was closed, just as she had left it. Taking a deep breath, she pushed it open.

The room was just as she remembered—dark, cluttered, and suffocating. Dust covered the surfaces, and books were piled high on the desk and shelves. Her father's notes, his research, were scattered everywhere, and the familiar sight made her heart ache.

She began searching, rifling through the papers and journals, looking for any mention of the ritual Isolde had spoken of. Time seemed to slip away as she worked, the weight of the house pressing down on her as the minutes stretched into hours.

And then she found it.

Tucked away in a forgotten drawer, beneath a pile of old, yellowed papers, was a leather-bound journal—older than anything else in the study. Its pages were worn and fragile, and as Elena opened it, the scent of ancient ink filled the air.

Her father's handwriting filled the pages, but this was different. This wasn't just his research. It was something more—something he had been hiding.

As she read, her heart pounded. The ritual, the curse, everything Isolde had said was true. Her father had been on the verge of breaking the curse, but he had run out of time. And now, it was up to her to finish what he had started.

But there was something else. Something darker.

In the final pages of the journal, her father had written about the Elder Vampire—about a bond that went deeper than she had realized. The ritual to break the curse wasn't just about severing the connection. It was about sacrifice.

To break the bond, Elena would have to destroy the source of the curse itself.

She would have to kill the Elder Vampire.

Chapter 17: The Price of Freedom

Elena stared at the final page of the journal, her hands trembling. The words blurred as her mind spun with the revelation. The ritual wasn't just about breaking the curse—it required her to kill the Elder Vampire. Her stomach twisted at the thought. He had taught her, guided her, even warned her about the dangers of the curse, but now she knew his true intention: he had been grooming her for his own ends.

To free herself, she had to destroy him. But the thought of confronting someone as powerful as the Elder Vampire seemed impossible. She had barely scratched the surface of what it meant to control her own hunger, let alone face him in a battle to the death.

The creak of a floorboard behind her snapped Elena from her thoughts. She spun around, her senses sharpened. The manor was empty—or so she had thought. But in the dim light of the study, she saw a figure emerging from the shadows.

Lucas.

"Lucas?" Her voice cracked with surprise, but relief flooded her. He was the one person who still felt like a tether to her old life, a life that now seemed so distant.

"I knew you'd be here," Lucas said, stepping into the room. His eyes scanned the study, the mess of papers and books strewn around her. "You've been avoiding me. What's going on, Elena? What's happening to you?"

Elena clenched her fists, feeling the gnawing hunger rise within her again, a constant presence in the back of her mind. She had been keeping her distance from him for a reason, and now that he was standing in front of her, it was harder to hide the truth.

"I didn't want you to get involved," she whispered, shaking her head. "This isn't your fight, Lucas."

Lucas stepped closer, concern etched across his face. "You don't get to make that decision for me. You're in danger, Elena. I can see it. Whatever this is, you're not alone. Let me help."

Tears pricked at the corners of her eyes. She wanted so badly to tell him everything, to unburden herself, but she couldn't bring him into this. Not when the stakes were so high. Not when the hunger inside her could turn her into a danger to him at any moment.

But Lucas wouldn't let it go. "You're hiding something, Elena. Please, just tell me. I can help you."

She took a deep breath, the weight of the truth pressing down on her. "I'm not who I used to be, Lucas. I'm… changing."

His brow furrowed, and he reached for her hand. "Changing how?"

"I'm turning into something else," Elena whispered. "Something dangerous."

Lucas's grip on her hand tightened, but he didn't pull away. "I don't care what's happening to you. You're still Elena to me."

Elena shook her head, tears slipping down her cheeks. "You don't understand. I have to stop the Elder Vampire. If I don't, I'll lose myself completely."

"The Elder Vampire?" Lucas's eyes widened, confusion and concern battling for dominance on his face. "Is this about the stories, the curse?"

Elena nodded; her voice barely audible. "He's been manipulating my family for centuries, and now he's using me. He wants me to complete a ritual that will give him full control. But I've found a way to stop him."

Lucas's jaw clenched. "Then we stop him. Together."

She bit her lip, holding back a sob. "It's not that simple. To break the curse, I have to kill him."

Lucas's eyes darkened as the weight of her words hit him. "And if you don't?"

"Then he'll complete the ritual," she said softly. "And I'll lose everything. My humanity, my soul—everything."

The room fell silent, the gravity of her words hanging between them. Lucas stepped closer, cupping her face in his hands. "We'll figure this out. You don't have to face this alone."

Elena's heart swelled with emotion. Lucas had always been her anchor, and now, in this darkest moment, he was still here, still willing to fight for her. But as much as she wanted to believe they could face this together, the reality was far more dangerous.

"I don't want to hurt you," she whispered, her voice shaking. "The hunger… it's getting stronger, Lucas. I can't control it."

Lucas didn't flinch. "Then I'll help you control it. I'm not leaving you."

Elena's chest tightened, but there was no time for hesitation. She wiped the tears from her face and nodded. "If you're really going to help me, we need to leave. Now. We have to find the ritual and prepare for what's coming."

Lucas nodded, his expression hardening with resolve. "Whatever it takes."

Chapter 18: Shadows Closing In

The two of them left Sinclair Manor under the cover of night. The air was thick with tension, every sound in the forest amplified as they made their way through the dark, winding path toward a destination Elena wasn't sure of. She knew they would need time to study her father's journal, to learn the counter-ritual that would sever the bond between her and the Elder Vampire. But the clock was ticking, and the danger was closing in.

As they walked in silence, Elena's heightened senses picked up every movement, every rustle of leaves, every heartbeat. She couldn't shake the feeling that they were being watched.

"I feel like someone's following us," Elena whispered, her eyes scanning the darkness.

Lucas looked around, his hand instinctively resting on the weapon he had brought with him. "Could it be him?"

"I don't know," Elena said, her voice tense. "But we need to move faster."

Just as she spoke, a gust of cold wind swept through the trees, sending a shiver down her spine. Something was wrong. The forest had gone unnaturally still, the usual sounds of wildlife suddenly absent.

Elena stopped, her heart racing. "Lucas, wait."

He turned to her; his brow furrowed. "What's wrong?"

Before she could answer, the shadows around them seemed to shift, moving as if they were alive. A dark figure stepped out from behind a cluster of trees, and Elena's breath caught in her throat.

It wasn't the Elder Vampire. It was someone else.

The figure was tall and cloaked in darkness, but there was a cold familiarity to his presence. As he stepped closer, the dim moonlight illuminated his face—a face Elena had seen in her darkest visions.

"It's been a long time, Elena," the figure said, his voice low and smooth. "I've been waiting for you."

Elena's blood turned to ice. "Who are you?"

The man's eyes glinted with a predatory gleam. "I'm someone who knows the truth about the Sinclair curse. And I've come to claim what's mine."

Lucas stepped forward, his hand gripping his weapon. "Stay back."

The man ignored him, his gaze fixed on Elena. "You've been misled, Elena. The Elder Vampire isn't the only one with power over your bloodline. There are others who want to see the curse broken—and I'm one of them."

Elena's pulse quickened, her heart pounding in her ears. "Who are you?"

"I am Sebastian," the man said, his voice dark and commanding. "And I'm here to offer you a choice."

Lucas narrowed his eyes. "What kind of choice?"

Sebastian's eyes flicked to Lucas for a brief moment before returning to Elena. "You can fight the Elder Vampire, kill him, and try to break the curse. Or… you can join me. Together, we can take control of the curse, bend it to our will. You can have the power you were always meant to wield, Elena."

Elena's stomach churned. "You want me to join you? Why?"

"Because I know what you're capable of," Sebastian said smoothly. "The Elder Vampire has been holding you back. He wants to use you, to trap you in his ancient schemes. But I can offer you freedom—real freedom. The kind that comes with power."

Elena clenched her fists, anger and confusion swirling inside her. "Why should I trust you?"

Sebastian's smile widened, a cold, calculating expression. "You shouldn't. But consider your options. Do you really think you can defeat the Elder Vampire on your own? He's been playing this game for centuries, and you're just a pawn. I can help you rise above that."

Elena's mind raced. Sebastian's words were tempting, but something about him felt wrong, dangerous. He was offering her power, but at what cost? And why now, after all these years, had he chosen to reveal himself?

Lucas stepped forward, his voice hard. "Whatever you're offering, we're not interested."

Sebastian's eyes flickered with amusement. "You think this is a choice for you, human?" He turned back to Elena, his voice softening. "This is your decision, Elena. Not his."

Elena's breath hitched. The weight of the moment pressed down on her, suffocating her. Sebastian's offer hung in the air like a poison, tempting her with promises of power and freedom, but the cost—the cost was too great.

"I won't join you," Elena said firmly, stepping back. "I'm going to stop the Elder Vampire, and I'm going to break the curse."

Sebastian's smile faded, his eyes darkening. "A foolish choice. But if that's your decision, I won't stop you." His voice lowered, a threat laced beneath the surface. "But know this, Elena—there are more players in this game than you realize. And I will be waiting when you fail."

With that, Sebastian disappeared into the shadows, leaving Elena and Lucas standing in the cold, oppressive silence of the forest.

Elena's chest heaved, her mind spinning. She had just rejected an offer of power, but the cost of that decision had yet to reveal itself. She turned to Lucas, her heart heavy with doubt.

"We need to keep moving," she whispered. "Before it's too late."

Chapter 19: The Ritual Begins

They reached a clearing deeper in the woods, far enough from the manor that Elena felt they had a moment to breathe. Her hands shook as she pulled her father's journal from her bag, flipping through the pages until she found the section detailing the counter-ritual.

The instructions were ancient, written in a language she barely understood. Her father had annotated the pages with translations and diagrams, but even with his notes, it seemed impossibly complex. She needed to prepare, to gather specific materials, to create the right conditions.

Lucas watched her with concern. "What do we need to do?"

Elena glanced up at him, her voice tight. "I need time to decipher this. We're going to have to perform the ritual soon, but if we're going to survive it—if I'm going to survive it—I need to understand everything first."

Lucas nodded, his hand on her shoulder. "We'll figure it out. You're not alone in this."

But as Elena looked down at the intricate instructions, she couldn't shake the feeling that time was running out. The Elder Vampire was close—she could feel it—and the hunger inside her was growing stronger, more insistent.

With each passing moment, the curse tightened its grip on her, and the clock ticked closer to midnight.

The ritual had begun.

Chapter 20: The Unraveling

As the clearing stretched in front of them, Elena felt a creeping sense of urgency rise within her. The stakes were higher than ever, and despite Lucas's steady presence beside her, she could feel the weight of something dark closing in. The forest was still, unnaturally so, as if holding its breath for what was to come.

Elena ran her fingers over the worn pages of her father's journal. Every diagram, every symbol felt like a piece of a puzzle, but one whose edges she couldn't quite grasp. The ritual was complex—far more complex than anything she had imagined. But something inside her had shifted. Doubt had crept in, and it had brought with it the shadow of a deeper truth: this was no longer a battle between good and evil. This was something else entirely.

"Maybe we're missing something," Lucas said, watching her closely. "If Sebastian knows so much about this, maybe—"

"No," Elena cut him off, shaking her head. "I don't trust him. He has his own agenda. Everyone does."

She felt the truth of her words settle deep in her chest. The Elder Vampire, Sebastian, even Isolde—each of them had played their part in this ancient game. She had been caught in their web, but now, for the first time, she was beginning to see the threads for what they were.

And yet, despite everything, one question gnawed at her: Was this truly her fight? Or had she inherited a battle that was never hers to begin with?

Suddenly, a thought struck her. "Maybe the curse... maybe the ritual... isn't about power. Maybe it's about something else."

Lucas frowned, stepping closer. "What do you mean?"

Elena's gaze drifted back to the journal. Her father's notes were frantic in the final pages, growing more desperate as he neared the end. The symbols became more obscure, more fragmented, as if he had discovered something that terrified him.

"I've been looking at this all wrong," she muttered, flipping through the pages. "This curse—it's not just about control or breaking a bond. It's about identity. It's about who we are—who I am."

Lucas's brow furrowed in confusion. "You mean… it's not just about the Elder Vampire?"

Elena shook her head, a cold clarity settling over her. "No. It's about me. The curse… it's tied to my bloodline, yes, but it's not about power—it's about survival. The Elder Vampire, Sebastian, even my father—they've all been trying to use me, use my family, to keep themselves alive. But maybe… maybe the curse is something deeper. Something that's meant to be transformed, not broken."

She flipped to a passage her father had written about the origins of the Sinclair curse. It was older than she had imagined, stretching back to a time when bloodlines were considered sacred, when curses weren't just about punishment—they were about evolution. Change.

"The ritual doesn't kill the Elder Vampire," Elena whispered, her eyes scanning the text. "It transforms him. It transforms *me*."

Lucas's eyes widened. "Transforms you into what?"

Elena's voice shook with realization. "Something neither vampire nor human. Something in between."

The gravity of the situation hit her like a wave. She had been fighting the hunger, the curse, the power within her—believing that to give in would mean losing herself. But now she realized that the battle wasn't about resisting. It was about accepting. Embracing. And in doing so, evolving into something entirely new.

"Lucas," she whispered, her voice filled with a strange calm. "The ritual isn't about killing the Elder Vampire. It's about merging with him. Becoming something different."

Lucas's face hardened. "You can't be serious. That's exactly what he wants—to take control of you."

"No," Elena said, shaking her head. "He doesn't know. He thinks this is about freeing himself. But this curse is older than him. It's older than all of us. It's a way to survive—to transcend."

Her words hung in the air, heavy with the weight of this new revelation. Lucas stared at her, his eyes full of concern. "You don't know what this could do to you. What if you lose yourself completely?"

Elena hesitated. The truth was, she didn't know. She had no idea what would happen if she followed through with the ritual, if she allowed the transformation to take place. But deep down, she knew this was the only way. To continue resisting the curse, to try to fight it, would only lead to more death, more destruction. But to embrace it, to allow the transformation—it could mean the end of the curse. The end of the centuries-old struggle.

"I don't have a choice," Elena said softly. "This is what I was meant for."

Lucas grabbed her arm, his eyes searching hers. "You always have a choice, Elena. Don't let them take that from you."

For a long moment, they stood in the clearing, the tension between them thick. Elena could see the fear in his eyes, but she could also see the unwavering loyalty, the determination to stand by her no matter what. And that made this decision even harder.

"I can't keep running from this," she said, her voice breaking. "If I don't do this, the cycle will never end. The Elder Vampire, Sebastian—they'll keep coming, keep using people, using me. But if I take control… maybe I can change it."

Lucas's grip tightened. "And what if you don't come back? What if this transformation—this merging—turns you into something you can't control?"

Elena met his gaze, her heart aching. "Then I'll need you to stop me."

Lucas's face fell, and his hand dropped from her arm. "Elena—"

Before he could finish, the forest around them shifted, the air growing colder. The darkness deepened, and Elena felt the familiar presence of the Elder Vampire closing in. She turned, her body tensing as the shadows coalesced into his figure.

The Elder Vampire stepped into the clearing; his red eyes gleaming in the moonlight. His expression was calm, controlled, but there was a flicker of something deeper in his gaze—a hunger that mirrored her own.

"Elena," he said softly, his voice like silk. "It's time."

Elena stood tall, her body thrumming with the power she had been resisting for so long. She could feel it now, flowing through her veins like fire, a part of her she had denied for too long.

"I know," she replied, her voice steady. "I know what you want."

The Elder Vampire smiled, a cold, predatory smile. "And you're ready to accept it?"

Elena stepped forward; the journal still clutched in her hands. "No. I'm ready to end it."

His smile faltered, confusion flashing across his face. "End it?"

Elena's eyes blazed with determination. "I'm not here to be your pawn. I'm not here to carry out your ritual. I'm here to take control."

The Elder Vampire's eyes narrowed. "You can't take control of something you don't understand, Elena. You're playing with forces far beyond your comprehension."

"Maybe," Elena said, her heart racing. "But this isn't just your curse. It's mine. And I'm not afraid of it anymore."

Before the Elder Vampire could respond, Elena lifted her father's journal, her voice rising with power. The words of the counter-ritual spilled from her lips, the ancient language flowing from her as though it had always been inside her.

The ground beneath them trembled, and the air around them crackled with energy. The Elder Vampire's face twisted in fury as he realized what was happening.

"Elena, you don't know what you're doing!" he snarled, stepping forward.

But Elena didn't stop. She kept chanting, her voice growing louder, stronger. The power surged through her, and she could feel the curse tightening around her like a coil, wrapping itself around her heart, her soul.

And then, with a final word, the ritual snapped into place.

The world around her exploded into light, and Elena felt herself being pulled into something far beyond her understanding.

The hunger, the power, the curse—it all consumed her, and for a moment, she was lost in it.

But then, just as quickly, she felt a shift. The power wasn't consuming her. It was merging with her. She wasn't becoming the Elder Vampire's vessel—she was becoming something else.

Something new.

Chapter 21: The Ascension

When the light faded and the world around her came back into focus, Elena found herself standing in the center of the clearing. But she was no longer the same.

Her senses were sharper, more attuned to the world around her. The hunger was still there, but it no longer controlled her. It was a part of her now, something she could wield, something she could shape.

The Elder Vampire stood before her, his expression one of shock and disbelief. He had expected her to be his vessel, his tool for breaking free of the curse. But now he saw the truth. The power he had sought to control had transformed Elena, not into his servant, but into something greater.

"You've… changed," he whispered, his voice filled with awe and fear.

Elena met his gaze, her eyes glowing with the power that now flowed through her. "Yes. And now, I'm ending this."

With a single motion, she raised her hand, and the Elder Vampire's body began to disintegrate before her eyes. He let out a final, desperate scream as he was consumed by the power of the curse that had bound him for centuries.

And then, he was gone. Reduced to nothing but ash.

Elena stood in the silence that followed, her chest rising and falling as the weight of what she had done settled over her. The curse, the hunger, the centuries-old battle—it was over.

Lucas stepped forward, his eyes wide with awe and fear. "Elena... what are you now?"

Elena turned to him; her heart heavy but her soul lighter than it had ever been. "I'm still me, Lucas. But I'm more than that now. I'm free."

She could see the worry in his eyes, the fear of what she had become. But as she took his hand, she smiled, feeling the power inside her settle, no longer wild, no longer uncontrollable.

For the first time in her life, Elena Sinclair was truly in control.

Chapter 22: Repercussions

Elena stood in the clearing, feeling the weight of the world lift from her shoulders. The power coursing through her was undeniable, yet different from the chaotic, uncontrolled force she had felt before. It was as if the curse had been redefined, not erased, and now she was something between human and vampire—something entirely her own. The Elder Vampire's ashes scattered at her feet, but the victory did not taste as sweet as she had imagined.

Lucas stood frozen, his eyes searching Elena's face for any sign of the woman he had once known. He took a step forward, his voice low. "What happens now?"

Elena turned to him, feeling the shift in her very being. "I don't know," she admitted softly, her voice carrying an unfamiliar resonance. "I've stopped him, but something's different now. I've changed."

Lucas hesitated, his eyes filled with a mix of awe and concern. "Elena, whatever you've done, it's not just power. It's something else." His voice trembled slightly as he added, "Are you still you?"

Elena swallowed hard, looking at her hands as if seeing them for the first time. She felt the cold edges of the transformation settle over her, but her mind, her soul—they still felt like her own. The hunger remained, quieter but present, no longer raging, but always there, whispering at the edges of her consciousness. It was not something she could ever ignore.

"I'm still me," she said, though a shadow of doubt flickered in her voice. "But I've become something more. Something I never wanted."

Lucas's brow furrowed. "You didn't want this, but now it's part of you. What does that mean? Is this really the end?"

Elena glanced at the remnants of the Elder Vampire, her thoughts racing. It should have been over, but deep down, she knew the game was far from finished. The curse might be transformed within her, but there were still lingering threads, old wounds that had yet to close. The power shift had left a ripple in the supernatural world—one she could feel in the air, like a disturbance that would attract more danger.

The clearing around them seemed to darken as if the night itself were pulling closer, watching her. She felt an unsettling presence, the weight of eyes that were not her own.

"There's more to this," Elena muttered, stepping away from the ashes. "Killing him wasn't the end. I can feel it."

Lucas's face darkened. "What do you mean? He's gone."

Elena took a breath, her senses heightened. "Yes, but his death created a vacuum. And power like this doesn't just disappear—it draws others in. Others like Sebastian."

The name hung in the air like a curse, and Lucas tensed at the mention of it. "Do you think he's coming for you?"

Elena shook her head. "Not just me. He wants more than that. He wants to control whatever's left of the curse. And now, I'm the only one who carries it."

For a moment, the weight of her words sank between them. Elena had feared the curse, resisted it, but now she was the bearer of something dangerous, something that would never leave her alone. She had broken free of the Elder Vampire's grasp, but she hadn't anticipated the new enemies this transformation would awaken.

"What do we do?" Lucas asked, his voice steady but laced with unease.

"We need to find Sebastian before he finds us," Elena said, her resolve hardening. "He's not the only one who'll want this power, but he's the one with the knowledge to use it. If he merges with the remnants of the curse, if he gets control of me... we're looking at something far worse than the Elder Vampire."

Chapter 23: The Hunt Begins

Days passed in a blur of preparation, strategy, and the creeping fear that they were being hunted. Elena and Lucas moved quickly, always one step ahead, but Elena could feel the strain. The transformation had given her more control over the hunger, but the constant balancing act between who she had been and what she had become was draining. She could sense the threads of power tugging at her, drawing her toward something darker, deeper, more ancient than the curse itself.

Sebastian was out there, somewhere in the shadows, waiting for his moment to strike.

Elena had poured over her father's journal again and again, searching for any hint of where Sebastian might hide or what his endgame truly was. The fragmented passages about old bloodlines and ancient rituals pointed to places of power, sites where the curse had been first born. And she knew that the answers she sought could only be found in one place: the catacombs beneath Sinclair Manor.

"I don't like this," Lucas muttered as they approached the decrepit estate once again. "It feels like a trap."

Elena nodded grimly. "It probably is. But it's the only way."

Sinclair Manor stood before them like a haunted relic of another era, its crumbling walls and darkened windows watching them with hollow eyes. Elena could feel the pull of the place, the bloodline that had bound her family to this curse for centuries, and now, it called her home.

She led the way through the overgrown garden and into the house, her senses alert to every sound, every shift in the air. The manor creaked under their footsteps, but there was something more—the faint echoes of a presence lurking just out of sight.

They descended into the catacombs beneath the estate, a labyrinth of stone tunnels that stretched deep into the earth. The air was cold, damp, and filled with the smell of decay. Elena's pulse quickened. She could feel Sebastian's presence, drawing nearer with every step.

As they reached the heart of the catacombs, an ancient chamber came into view, its walls lined with strange symbols and relics that predated her family's history. In the center of the chamber stood an altar, and Sebastian.

He was waiting for them.

"I knew you'd come," Sebastian said, his voice echoing off the stone walls. "You couldn't resist the pull of your bloodline. It's in your nature."

Elena stepped forward, her heart pounding in her chest. "This ends now, Sebastian. You won't take control of the curse."

Sebastian's lips curved into a slow smile; his eyes gleaming with dark amusement. "Take control? No, Elena. I don't want to control the curse. I want to reshape it. To make it something greater than it ever was."

Elena's stomach twisted. "You want to merge with it. With me."

Sebastian nodded, his gaze intense. "Together, we can break the limits of the curse. You've felt it, haven't you? The power that comes with the transformation. But it's only a fraction of what's possible. If we unite, we can transcend it all—vampire, human, everything."

Lucas stepped forward; his jaw clenched. "You're out of your mind. She won't let you."

Sebastian's eyes flicked to Lucas, his smile widening. "You're the outsider here. You have no idea what's at stake. This isn't just about her—it's about the future of our kind."

Elena's hands balled into fists; her voice steady but filled with conviction. "I don't want your future, Sebastian. I'm not going to become what you are."

Sebastian's smile faded, his expression hardening. "You don't have a choice, Elena. You are the last of the Sinclair line. You carry the curse, and it will either destroy you or evolve you. The question is—will you fight it and fail, or will you rise above it and become something more?"

For a brief moment, doubt flickered in Elena's mind. She had fought so hard to control the curse, to understand it, but now, standing in this ancient place, she could feel the pull of something greater. The curse wasn't just a burden—it was power. And it wanted to be used.

"I won't become you," she said softly, but her voice wavered, the weight of the decision pressing down on her.

Sebastian took a step forward, his eyes gleaming. "You already have."

Before she could respond, the chamber erupted into chaos. Shadows moved, ancient symbols on the walls began to glow with a dark energy, and the ground beneath their feet trembled. Sebastian raised his arms, chanting in a language Elena had never heard but instinctively understood. The curse was awakening, and Sebastian was calling it to him.

"Elena!" Lucas shouted, drawing his weapon, but before he could move, the shadows wrapped around him, pinning him to the ground.

Elena felt the power surge through her, and for a moment, she was lost in it. The curse called to her, its voice seductive, promising power beyond anything she had ever imagined. She could end it all here. She could merge with the curse, with Sebastian, and become something more than either of them had ever dreamed.

But in that moment, she remembered her father's journal—the warnings he had left, the desperate notes scrawled in the margins. The curse wasn't about power. It was about destruction. If she gave in, she wouldn't evolve. She would lose everything.

With a scream, Elena fought back against the pull of the curse, channeling all of her strength into a single, focused burst of power. The shadows recoiled, the energy in the chamber dimmed, and Sebastian staggered, his eyes wide with shock.

"No," Elena said, her voice steady now. "This ends with me."

And with a final surge of power, she unleashed the full force of the curse—not to control it, but to destroy it. The ancient symbols on the walls shattered, the ground cracked beneath them, and the curse—the centuries-old curse that had plagued her family—disintegrated into nothing.

Sebastian screamed as he was consumed by the very power he had sought to control. His body dissolved into ash, leaving only silence in the chamber.

Elena collapsed to the ground; the weight of the curse finally lifted from her. She was free.

Chapter 24: A New Dawn

When Elena awoke, the sun was rising above the trees, casting a warm, golden light over the landscape. The air felt fresh, clean, and for the first time in her life, she felt truly at peace.

She and Lucas had made it out of the catacombs, barely escaping the collapse of the chamber. The curse was gone, and with it, the dark legacy that had haunted her family for centuries.

Elena stood at the edge of the clearing, watching the sun rise. The hunger inside her was gone, replaced by a quiet sense of calm. She had defeated the curse, but more importantly, she had defeated the part of herself that had been afraid to embrace who she was.

Lucas stepped up beside her, his face still bruised from the battle, but his eyes filled with relief. "It's over, isn't it?"

Elena nodded, her heart light. "It's over."

They stood in silence for a moment, watching the new day unfold before them. The world felt different, full of possibility, and for the first time in a long time, Elena felt like she had a future. One that was hers to shape, free from the shadow of the curse.

"What will you do now?" Lucas asked, his voice soft.

Elena smiled, feeling the warmth of the sun on her skin. "I don't know. But whatever it is, it'll be my choice."

She had been through darkness and back again, but now, as the sun rose over Sinclair Manor, she knew that this was her beginning. And for the first time, she wasn't afraid.

Chapter 25: Shadows of the Past

Elena sat in the dark study of Sinclair Manor, the musty scent of old books and forgotten memories filling the air. Her father's journal lay open in front of her, its pages yellowed with time. The house had been silent for years, but now that she was back, the walls seemed to hum with the weight of her family's history. The journal entries, scrawled in her father's tight, frantic handwriting, were filled with cryptic references to the curse, to the Elder Vampire, and to something deeper—something she had never fully understood.

Her father had known more than he had let on. He had spent years researching the origins of the curse, tracking its roots back to an ancestor named Lucius Sinclair. Elena's fingers traced the edge of the journal as she thought about Lucius, the man who had made the pact that had cursed their bloodline for centuries.

"Elena?"

Lucas's voice broke through the silence, and she looked up to find him standing in the doorway, his face etched with concern. He had been watching her closely since their last encounter with Sebastian. He was always watching now, waiting for something to change in her.

She managed a small smile, though her mind was still preoccupied with the weight of the journal's revelations. "I'm okay. Just… thinking."

Lucas stepped into the room, his presence grounding her in a way nothing else could. He was a constant in the chaos of her life, but even now, she could sense the distance growing between them. The transformation had changed her, and no matter how much he wanted to believe she was still the same, they both knew that wasn't entirely true.

He sat down across from her, his gaze shifting to the open journal. "What did you find?"

Elena hesitated for a moment before answering. "It's about Lucius Sinclair. My father wrote about him—about how the curse started. I always knew there was more to the story, but this… this is different. It's darker than I thought."

Lucas frowned, leaning in to look at the journal's pages. "Darker how?"

She flipped to an entry she had read earlier that day. Her father had written about an ancient ceremony, a ritual that Lucius had performed centuries ago. It had been the beginning of everything, the pact that had bound their bloodline to the Elder Vampire. But what caught Elena's attention was the mention of another figure—a woman, someone Lucius had trusted, someone who had betrayed him in the end.

"Elisabeth," Elena said softly, her fingers brushing over the name. "She was a part of the ritual. My father's notes are incomplete, but it looks like she was supposed to help Lucius seal the pact. Instead, she turned on him. And whatever she did... it twisted the curse. Made it more powerful."

Lucas's brow furrowed. "You think this Elisabeth had something to do with the curse becoming what it is today?"

"I don't know," Elena admitted. "But it seems like she played a bigger role than we thought. My father believed that if we could understand what happened during that ritual, we might be able to undo it."

Lucas leaned back in his chair; his eyes fixed on Elena. "So what does this mean for you?"

Elena sighed, closing the journal. "It means I need to know more. If there's any chance of breaking the curse or changing it… I have to find out what happened to Lucius and Elisabeth. I need to understand their connection to the Elder Vampire."

Lucas nodded, though she could see the worry in his eyes. "We'll figure it out. Together."

She gave him a grateful smile, but deep down, Elena knew this was something she had to face on her own. No matter how much Lucas wanted to help, the curse was hers to bear, and the answers lay buried in the past.

Chapter 26: Echoes of the Ancestors

Later that night, Elena found herself standing in the manor's library, surrounded by the forgotten relics of her family's long and troubled history. The air was thick with dust, and the shelves were lined with books and artifacts that had been collected over the centuries by generations of Sinclairs. Many of these items were older than the house itself, some passed down from Lucius's time.

She had come to the library searching for clues—something that might tell her more about Elisabeth and the role she had played in the curse. Her father's journal had only scratched the surface, and Elena knew there had to be more hidden within the manor's walls.

As she searched through the shelves, her fingers brushed against an old leather-bound book, its spine cracked with age. Pulling it free from its place, she opened it to find a family tree—a record of the Sinclair bloodline, going back centuries.

Her eyes scanned the names, following the branches back to the time of Lucius Sinclair. His name was listed near the top, along with the names of his children and descendants. But as she looked closer, she noticed something strange. Next to Lucius's name, there was another name—one that had been crossed out.

"Elisabeth," Elena whispered.

The ink had faded, but the name was still legible, etched into the page like a ghost from the past. This was her, the woman who had betrayed Lucius during the ritual. But why had her name been erased? What had happened to her after the curse had been unleashed?

"Elena."

She turned at the sound of the voice, but the room was empty. For a moment, she thought it had been Lucas calling to her, but there was no one there.

"Elena."

The voice came again, soft and haunting, like a whisper carried on the wind. Her heart raced, and she felt a chill run down her spine. It was a woman's voice; one she had never heard before.

She glanced around the room, her senses on high alert. The air seemed to grow colder, and the shadows in the corners of the library shifted, moving as if they were alive.

"Elisabeth?" Elena called out, her voice trembling.

The voice didn't answer, but the presence remained, lingering in the room like a ghost. Elena closed the book, her hands shaking. There was something—someone—trying to reach her. And she knew that whatever it was, it was tied to the curse.

She gathered her courage and left the library, her mind racing with questions. If Elisabeth was trying to contact her, it could mean that there were still pieces of the puzzle she hadn't uncovered. And if that was the case, she needed to find out what role Elisabeth had truly played in Lucius's downfall—and how it connected to her own fate.

Chapter 27: Fractures in Time

That night, Elena dreamed.

In her dream, she stood in a grand hall, its walls adorned with tapestries depicting ancient battles and scenes of power. The room was lit by flickering torches, casting long shadows across the stone floor. In the center of the hall, a tall man stood with his back to her, his posture rigid and commanding. She knew instantly who he was.

Lucius Sinclair.

He was dressed in ornate clothing from a time long past, his hands clasped behind his back as he stared at something beyond the far wall. Elena took a step forward, her heart pounding in her chest. She wanted to call out to him, to warn him, but the words stuck in her throat.

As she moved closer, she saw the figure of a woman standing beside Lucius. Her hair was dark, her features sharp and beautiful. She wore a long, flowing gown that shimmered in the dim light, and her eyes—Elena recognized them instantly.

Elisabeth.

The two figures spoke in hushed tones, their words inaudible to Elena, but the tension between them was palpable. Lucius turned to face her, his expression hard, filled with anger and betrayal. Elisabeth's face remained calm, her gaze unwavering as she held his.

Suddenly, the scene shifted. The grand hall dissolved, and Elena found herself standing in the middle of a dark forest, the trees towering above her like sentinels. The air was thick with the scent of earth and decay, and the ground beneath her feet was slick with mud. She could hear the sound of footsteps in the distance, growing louder with each passing moment.

"Elena…"

The voice was closer now, and this time, she knew it was real.

Elisabeth's figure appeared before her, shimmering like a mirage. Her dark eyes locked onto Elena's, and in that moment, she felt the weight of centuries pressing down on her. The curse, the betrayal, the power—it all flowed from Elisabeth, and Elena understood now what had happened.

"You are not like him," Elisabeth whispered, her voice soft but filled with a strange intensity. "You can change what he could not."

Elena's breath caught in her throat. "What do you mean?"

Elisabeth stepped closer, her presence both unsettling and compelling. "The curse is not a weapon. It is a key. Lucius believed it would grant him power, but he was wrong. It will destroy those who seek to control it. But you, Elena… you can set it free."

Before Elena could respond, the vision shattered, and she awoke with a gasp, her heart pounding in her chest. She sat up in bed, her mind racing with the fragments of the dream.

"Elena?" Lucas's voice came from the doorway, and she looked up to find him standing there, his face filled with concern. "Are you okay?"

She took a deep breath, trying to steady herself. "I think... I think I understand now."

Lucas frowned, stepping into the room. "Understand what?"

"The curse," she said softly, her voice trembling. "It's not about control. It's about freedom. It's about breaking the chains that bind us."

Lucas's brow furrowed. "What are you saying?"

Elena looked up at him, her eyes filled with a new sense of purpose. "I know what I have to do now. I have to finish what Lucius couldn't. I have to free us all."

Chapter 28: The Factions Awaken

The morning light had barely touched the windows of Sinclair Manor when Elena felt the first stirrings of danger. It was subtle at first—a faint vibration in the air, an uneasy sensation creeping into her bones. She had been working tirelessly to unravel the mystery of Elisabeth and Lucius, but now something was pulling her away from that search, something pressing and immediate.

As she descended the grand staircase, Lucas met her at the bottom, his face tense.

"They're coming," he said quietly.

Elena frowned. "Who?"

"Vampires. Not just a few. A lot." Lucas's voice was steady, but the concern in his eyes was unmistakable. "I think word's gotten out that you… killed the Elder Vampire."

Her stomach dropped. It had been days since the confrontation in the catacombs, and though she had sensed a shift in the supernatural balance, she hadn't anticipated how quickly others would take notice.

"Sebastian," she muttered under her breath. She had expected him to make a move, but she hadn't realized that his influence extended so far.

"There's more," Lucas continued, pulling her further into the hall, away from the open windows. "I did some digging. It turns out Sebastian isn't just another vampire. He's part of something bigger—a faction that's been vying for control ever since the Elder Vampire went underground. Now that the curse is in flux, they see an opportunity."

Elena's mind raced. "A faction?"

Lucas nodded. "They're called the **Sanguis Ascendancy**, and they're not the only ones. There are others too—groups that have been waiting in the shadows, waiting for a shift in power. You killing the Elder Vampire might have just set off a chain reaction."

Elena's heart pounded. The curse had always been a personal battle, something she had fought to understand and control. But now, it seemed that the curse was more than just a family legacy. It was the key to something much larger—a power struggle that had been brewing for centuries.

"We need to figure out what they want," Elena said, her voice steady despite the tension building in her chest. "If they're coming here, it's because they think they can use me."

Lucas clenched his jaw. "Exactly. You're the last link to the curse. Whoever controls you, controls everything."

A cold chill ran down Elena's spine. The weight of responsibility was suffocating, but there was no turning back now. If she was going to face the factions, she needed to be ready.

"What do we do?" Lucas asked, his voice low.

Elena took a deep breath. "We don't wait for them to come to us. We go to them."

Chapter 29: The Council of Shadows

Elena and Lucas traveled north to a location that Lucas's sources had uncovered—a centuries-old estate hidden deep in the forest, where the vampire factions were rumored to meet. As they approached, Elena could feel the ancient energy of the place, a pulse of power that resonated with the curse inside her.

The estate was massive, its towering walls covered in ivy and its windows darkened, reflecting the clouded sky. There was a sense of dread in the air, as though the building itself had witnessed horrors beyond imagination.

As they entered the estate's grounds, they were met by a figure draped in a long, dark cloak, his face obscured by a hood.

"Elena Sinclair," the figure said, his voice smooth but cold. "We've been expecting you."

Elena didn't flinch. "Take me to them."

The figure nodded and turned, leading them through the grand entrance and into the depths of the estate. The interior was just as foreboding as the exterior—dark wood paneling, flickering candles casting long shadows, and walls lined with portraits of long-dead vampires.

They were led into a large hall, where a group of figures sat around a long, ornate table. Each one wore a different symbol, marking their allegiance to various factions. At the head of the table sat Sebastian, his eyes gleaming with amusement.

"Elena," Sebastian said, spreading his arms wide as if welcoming an old friend. "I'm glad you could join us."

Elena's eyes narrowed. "I didn't come here to play games, Sebastian."

Sebastian's smile widened. "Oh, but this is no game. This is a war."

He gestured to the other vampires at the table. "The Sangu is Ascendancy, the **Order of the Forgotten**, and even the **Night born Syndicate**—they're all here because of you. You've changed the balance of power, Elena. And now, everyone wants a piece of what's left."

Elena's pulse quickened, but she kept her voice calm. "And what do you want?"

Sebastian leaned forward; his eyes gleaming. "To survive. To thrive. You have something we all need—the key to controlling the curse. But more than that, you have the power to reshape what we are."

Elena's stomach twisted. "I'm not a tool for your power games."

Sebastian's smile faded. "No. You're not. You're more than that. You're the future."

The other vampires at the table murmured amongst themselves, their eyes flicking between Sebastian and Elena. She could feel the tension rising in the room, the weight of centuries-old rivalries bubbling beneath the surface.

One of the vampires, a woman with sharp, angular features and a scar across her cheek, spoke up. "If we let her control the curse, who's to say she won't turn on all of us?"

Sebastian's gaze flicked to her, and he raised an eyebrow. "Would you rather leave it in the hands of the humans? Or worse, see it die out altogether?"

The woman's lips pressed into a thin line, but she said nothing.

Elena stepped forward; her voice strong. "I didn't come here to join any of you. I came here to put an end to this."

Sebastian's eyes darkened. "And how do you intend to do that?"

Elena took a deep breath, her mind racing with everything she had learned—about Lucius, Elisabeth, the curse, and its true nature. "The curse was never meant to give you power. It was meant to free us. But you've twisted it into something monstrous."

Sebastian's lips curled into a sneer. "You don't understand the curse, Elena. Not like I do. It's not something you can simply 'end.' It's part of us now."

Elena met his gaze, unflinching. "I'm going to break it."

The room fell silent, the vampires around the table staring at her in shock. Sebastian's smile returned, but this time it was colder, more menacing.

"You think you can break the curse?" he asked, his voice dripping with condescension. "You think you can undo what was done centuries ago?"

Elena's heart pounded, but she stood her ground. "I know I can."

Before Sebastian could respond, the doors to the hall burst open, and a figure strode in—a woman with striking white hair and eyes that glowed faintly in the dim light.

Isolde.

"Elena's right," Isolde said, her voice carrying an authority that silenced the room. "The curse can be broken. But it will take more than just power. It will take sacrifice."

Elena's breath caught in her throat as Isolde's eyes met hers. There was something different about her, something Elena hadn't seen before. Isolde wasn't just a rogue vampire trying to escape the curse—she was part of something much larger.

Sebastian's eyes narrowed as he looked at Isolde. "You think you can break the curse? After all this time?"

Isolde stepped forward, her gaze hard. "I know how to break it. But it's not just about Elena. It's about all of us."

The room fell into tense silence as Isolde's words hung in the air. The factions had been fighting for control, for power, but now they were faced with a new possibility—one that none of them had anticipated.

Elena turned to Isolde; her voice quiet but filled with determination. "What do we have to do?"

Isolde's eyes softened, but there was a flicker of sadness in them. "To break the curse, someone must return to the beginning. Someone must go back to where it all started."

Elena frowned, confusion washing over her. "What do you mean?"

Isolde's gaze drifted to the table, to the symbols carved into the wood. "Lucius wasn't the only one involved in the ritual that created the curse. Elisabeth's role was just as important. If we want to break the curse, we have to go back to the place where the ritual was performed and reverse what was done."

Sebastian scoffed. "You're talking about a myth. That place doesn't exist anymore."

Isolde's eyes flicked to him, cold and unwavering. "It exists. And we have to find it."

Elena's heart pounded in her chest. The weight of what Isolde was saying began to sink in. This wasn't just about breaking the curse—it was about going back to the moment when it all began. And if they failed, the consequences would be unimaginable.

"Where do we start?" Elena asked, her voice steady.

Isolde turned to her, her expression grave. "We start by finding the place where Lucius and Elisabeth performed the original ritual. And we need to do it before the factions tear each other apart."

Chapter 30: Lucas's Dilemma

As the meeting with the vampire factions ended and they left the estate, Lucas walked alongside Elena in silence. The tension between them had been growing ever since they had entered this world of ancient bloodlines and power struggles. He had been trying to stay by her side, to be the one she could trust. But now, more than ever, he felt like an outsider in her world.

Elena could feel his unease, the questions that he hadn't asked but were always present in his gaze. She had changed, and Lucas was struggling to accept what she had become.

"You're quiet," Elena said softly, glancing at him.

Lucas ran a hand through his hair, his brow furrowed. "I'm just trying to wrap my head around all of this. I mean, factions? Rituals? Breaking an ancient curse?" He shook his head, his voice strained. "It feels like we're in over our heads."

Elena nodded, understanding his frustration. "I know it's a lot. But I need you with me, Lucas. I need someone I can trust."

Lucas stopped walking, turning to face her. "And I'm here, Elena. But…" He hesitated, his voice trailing off.

"But what?"

He took a deep breath, his eyes searching hers. "But I don't know if I can do this. I don't know if I can watch you… become something I don't recognize."

Elena's chest tightened. She had always known that this would be a possibility, that the changes she had undergone might push Lucas away. But hearing him say it out loud brought a sharp pain to her heart.

"I'm still me," she said quietly, her voice trembling.

Lucas shook his head. "Are you? I want to believe that. I really do. But the more you dive into this world, the more I feel like I'm losing you."

Elena swallowed hard, tears pricking at the corners of her eyes. "I'm trying to stop this, Lucas. I'm trying to break the curse. If I don't, I'll lose myself completely."

Lucas's face softened, but the sadness in his eyes remained. "And what if breaking the curse means becoming something else? Something I don't recognize?"

Elena didn't have an answer. She had been so focused on fighting the curse, on finding a way to end it, that she hadn't fully considered what the cost might be. And now, standing here with Lucas, she realized just how high that cost could be.

"I don't know," she whispered, her voice breaking. "But I have to try."

Lucas stepped closer, cupping her face in his hands. "I'll be with you, Elena. I'll fight with you. But I'm scared. I'm scared of losing you."

Tears slipped down her cheeks as she leaned into his touch. "I'm scared too."

For a moment, they stood there in silence, the weight of their fears pressing down on them. But despite the uncertainty, despite the danger, they knew they couldn't turn back now.

The battle was just beginning, and they would face it together—no matter what the future held.

Chapter 31: The Journey

Elena and Lucas stood at the edge of a vast, foreboding forest as the sun dipped below the horizon, casting long shadows across the land. The air was thick with the scent of damp earth and ancient wood, and a cold wind whispered through the trees, carrying with it the faint echoes of the past. They had left the vampire factions behind, at least for now, but their mission was far from over.

Beside them, Isolde surveyed the landscape with a quiet intensity, her white hair catching the fading light. She had been guiding them ever since the encounter with the factions, leading them toward the place where it had all begun—the site of the original ritual that had bound the Sinclair bloodline to the curse.

"This is it," Isolde said, her voice low. "We're close."

Elena stared into the darkening woods, a knot of tension tightening in her chest. She had been preparing for this moment, the final leg of their journey, but the weight of what lay ahead still pressed heavily on her shoulders. Somewhere in the depths of that forest lay the answers they sought—and the dangers they could not yet fathom.

Lucas shifted beside her; his face tight with concern. "What exactly are we walking into, Isolde? What's out there?"

Isolde's eyes flicked toward him; her expression unreadable. "It's not what's out there that you should be worried about. It's what you'll find within."

Elena's stomach twisted. "What do you mean?"

Isolde sighed, turning her gaze back to the forest. "This place… it's more than just the site of the ritual. It's a place of power. A place where the curse was born, and where it will either be broken or strengthened. What we face here will be as much about confronting the past as it is about confronting the curse itself."

Elena felt a chill run down her spine. She had come this far, fought so many battles, but this was different. The curse had been a looming presence in her life, something she had tried to fight, control, or escape. But now she would face it directly, in the place where it had all begun.

"We have no choice," Elena said softly, her voice steady despite the fear gnawing at her insides. "If we don't break the curse here, it will consume me."

Lucas stepped closer to her, his hand brushing hers, a silent reassurance that he was still with her. She looked up at him, their eyes meeting for a brief moment, and in that exchange, Elena found the strength to continue.

Isolde nodded, satisfied with their resolve. "We move at first light."

Chapter 32: The Journey Begins

Elena and Lucas stood at the edge of a vast, foreboding forest as the sun dipped below the horizon, casting long shadows across the land. The air was thick with the scent of damp earth and ancient wood, and a cold wind whispered through the trees, carrying with it the faint echoes of the past. They had left the vampire factions behind, at least for now, but their mission was far from over.

Beside them, Isolde surveyed the landscape with a quiet intensity, her white hair catching the fading light. She had been guiding them ever since the encounter with the factions, leading them toward the place where it had all begun—the site of the original ritual that had bound the Sinclair bloodline to the curse.

"This is it," Isolde said, her voice low. "We're close."

Elena stared into the darkening woods, a knot of tension tightening in her chest. She had been preparing for this moment, the final leg of their journey, but the weight of what lay ahead still pressed heavily on her shoulders. Somewhere in the depths of that forest lay the answers they sought—and the dangers they could not yet fathom.

Lucas shifted beside her; his face tight with concern. "What exactly are we walking into, Isolde? What's out there?"

Isolde's eyes flicked toward him, her expression unreadable. "It's not what's out there that you should be worried about. It's what you'll find within."

Elena's stomach twisted. "What do you mean?"

Isolde sighed, turning her gaze back to the forest. "This place… it's more than just the site of the ritual. It's a place of power. A place where the curse was born, and where it will either be broken or strengthened. What we face here will be as much about confronting the past as it is about confronting the curse itself."

Elena felt a chill run down her spine. She had come this far, fought so many battles, but this was different. The curse had been a looming presence in her life, something she had tried to fight, control, or escape. But now she would face it directly, in the place where it had all begun.

"We have no choice," Elena said softly, her voice steady despite the fear gnawing at her insides. "If we don't break the curse here, it will consume me."

Lucas stepped closer to her, his hand brushing hers, a silent reassurance that he was still with her. She looked up at him, their eyes meeting for a brief moment, and in that exchange, Elena found the strength to continue.

Isolde nodded, satisfied with their resolve. "We move at first light."

Chapter 33: A Place of Power

At dawn, the three of them ventured deeper into the forest, the trees closing in around them like towering sentinels. The air was cold and heavy, and Elena could feel the weight of the place pressing down on her, as if the land itself carried the burden of centuries of magic and blood. The further they went, the more the forest seemed to transform—growing darker, the trees gnarled and twisted, the very ground beneath their feet soft and shifting.

It didn't take long before they reached the heart of the forest, a clearing ringed with massive, ancient stones, each one inscribed with strange, indecipherable runes. The air here was different charged with a dark, powerful energy that made Elena's skin prickle. This was the place where the original ritual had been performed.

"Elena," Isolde said, her voice softer now. "This is where Lucius and Elisabeth attempted to unlock the full power of the curse."

Elena swallowed hard, stepping into the clearing. Her heart raced as she looked around, the runes on the stones flickering faintly with a residual energy that seemed to recognize her. She had expected to feel anger, fear, or even regret standing here, but what she felt most of all was a deep connection—like she belonged here, like she was meant to finish what had been started centuries ago.

"This is where I break the curse," Elena whispered, more to herself than to the others. She could feel it, deep in her bones. The curse wasn't just something inflicted upon her—it was something tied to her, something that had become a part of her very essence. And now, in this place of power, she would face it head-on.

But as she stepped closer to the center of the clearing, a shadow fell over her. She froze, her senses going on high alert.

They weren't alone.

Lucas tensed, his hand moving instinctively toward his weapon. "What is it?"

Before Elena could answer, a figure emerged from the trees—a figure she had been dreading. Sebastian.

He stepped into the clearing with the confidence of someone who had been expecting this moment all along. His dark eyes gleamed with amusement as he looked at Elena, then at the ancient stones that surrounded them.

"You didn't think you could break the curse without me, did you?" he said, his voice smooth and mocking.

Elena's fists clenched at her sides. "This has nothing to do with you."

Sebastian's smile widened. "Oh, but it does. You see, Elena, the curse isn't just your burden to bear. It's ours. It's all of ours. And you—" He pointed at her, his eyes narrowing. "You're the key to unlocking its full potential."

Elena's heart pounded. "I'm not going to help you gain more power."

Sebastian laughed, a cold, humorless sound. "Power? You still think this is about power?

No, Elena. This is about survival. For all of us. The curse is changing. It's evolving. And if you don't embrace what it is, what we are, then it will destroy you."

Isolde stepped forward; her face grim. "She doesn't have to listen to you, Sebastian. The curse can be broken."

Sebastian's eyes flicked to Isolde, his expression darkening. "You always were naive, Isolde. The curse can't be broken. It can only be controlled."

Elena shook her head. "You're wrong. I've seen it. I've felt it. The curse isn't just something to control—it's something that can be freed."

Sebastian's smile faded, his gaze hardening. "Then you're a fool."

Without warning, the ground beneath them trembled, and the air around the clearing seemed to vibrate with dark energy. The stones flickered, their runes glowing brighter as the power of the curse awakened. Elena felt it surge through her, a wave of raw energy that made her knees buckle.

"Elena!" Lucas called out, reaching for her, but the energy was too strong, too overwhelming.

She stumbled forward, her vision blurring as the curse wrapped itself around her, pulling her toward the center of the clearing. She could hear the voices now—the whispers of the past, of Lucius and Elisabeth, of those who had come before her, all of them speaking as one.

"Elena…"

The voice was distant, yet familiar, echoing through the clearing like a forgotten memory. It was Lucius, she realized, his presence woven into the very fabric of the curse. And with him, she could feel Elisabeth—a force just as powerful, just as present.

They were here. They had always been here.

"Elena…"

The power surged again, and this time, she let it in. She didn't resist. She couldn't. The curse was a part of her, and in this place of power, it was stronger than ever. But this time, instead of fighting it, she embraced it.

For so long, she had feared the curse, feared what it would make her become. But now she understood. The curse wasn't just about blood or power. It was about transformation. It was about freedom.

"Elena!" Lucas shouted again; his voice filled with fear.

But Elena was no longer afraid.

She stood tall in the center of the clearing, her eyes glowing with the energy of the curse. She could feel it coursing through her veins, but this time, it didn't consume her. It didn't control her. It was hers.

And as she looked up at Sebastian, she knew what had to be done.

Chapter 34: The Final Confrontation

Sebastian's eyes narrowed as he watched Elena rise to her full power. The smile that had been on his face was gone, replaced by a dark, simmering anger. He had underestimated her, and now he was beginning to realize the true scope of what she had become.

"Elena," Sebastian said, his voice low and dangerous. "You don't know what you're doing."

But Elena did know. She knew exactly what she was doing.

"I'm ending this," she said, her voice steady, the power in her voice reverberating through the clearing.

Sebastian stepped forward, his expression twisting with fury. "You think you can stop me? You think you can break the curse?"

Elena's gaze was unwavering. "I know I can."

With a roar of fury, Sebastian lunged toward her, his form shifting as he unleashed the full force of his vampiric power. The ground beneath them cracked, and the air around them swirled with dark energy as the curse surged through the clearing.

But Elena was ready. She had embraced the curse, made it her own, and now she wielded it with a strength that far surpassed anything Sebastian could have imagined.

She raised her hand, and the energy of the curse flowed from her, striking Sebastian with a force that sent him crashing to the ground. He screamed in agony as the power of the curse tore through him, unraveling the dark magic that had bound him for centuries.

But Sebastian wasn't done yet. He staggered to his feet, his body trembling with rage and pain. "You... will... not... defeat... me!"

Elena's eyes blazed with power as she stepped forward. "I already have."

With a final burst of energy, Elena unleashed the full force of the curse, and Sebastian's body was consumed by the dark magic he had sought to control. His screams echoed through the clearing as his form dissolved into ash, leaving nothing behind but the faint whisper of his defeat.

The ground stilled, and the air grew quiet. The power of the curse ebbed, its dark energy receding as Elena stood in the center of the clearing, her chest heaving with the weight of what she had done.

It was over.

Isolde stepped forward, her face a mixture of awe and relief. "You did it, Elena. You've broken the curse."

But as Elena looked down at her hands, the power still humming beneath her skin, she knew that breaking the curse hadn't freed her. It had transformed her. She was no longer bound by the curse, but she was still its keeper. The bloodline had changed, and with it, so had she.

"Elena?" Lucas's voice was soft, hesitant.

She turned to him, her heart aching at the look in his eyes. He had been with her through everything, but now, standing before him, she wasn't the same person he had once known. She had become something more—something that could no longer fit into the world she had left behind.

"I'm still me," she said softly, but even as she spoke the words, she knew they weren't entirely true.

Lucas nodded, but the sadness in his eyes told her he understood. "I know."

For a moment, they stood there in silence, the weight of the past and the uncertainty of the future hanging between them. But despite the distance that had grown between them, they were still connected—by the journey they had shared, by the battles they had fought together, and by the love that still lingered in the spaces between their words.

"What happens now?" Lucas asked quietly.

Elena looked up at the sky, the first light of dawn breaking through the trees. She didn't know what the future held, but she knew one thing for certain.

"This is just the beginning."

Chapter 35: A New Dawn

As the first rays of sunlight broke over the horizon, Elena stood at the edge of the clearing, the wind tugging gently at her hair. The curse was broken, its dark energy dissipated into the earth, but the sense of finality that she had expected didn't come. Instead, there was a quiet, lingering presence—a reminder that though the battle was over, the consequences of her actions were just beginning.

Isolde stood beside her, silent for a long time before she spoke. "You've done what no one thought possible. You've ended the curse. But

ded, her gaze fixed on the distant horizon. "I know. And I don't know what you've also changed everything."

Elena nodded that means yet."

Isolde turned to face her; her expression unreadable. "The power inside you… it's still there. It will always be a part of you now."

"I can feel it," Elena said softly. "It's different, though. It's not something I have to fight anymore. It's just… me."

Isolde gave a slight nod of understanding. "You're something new, Elena. You've become more than a Sinclair, more than a vampire. What you do with that power is up to you."

Elena looked at Isolde, her heart heavy with the weight of that truth. "And what about you? What will you do?"

Isolde's eyes softened, a rare flicker of warmth crossing her face. "I've been fighting this battle for centuries. Maybe it's time I find something else to fight for."

Elena smiled, grateful for the bond they had formed, even amidst the chaos. Isolde had guided her through the darkest parts of her journey, and now it was time for both of them to find a new path.

As the sun climbed higher in the sky, Elena turned to Lucas, who stood a few feet away, watching her with quiet intensity. There was so much left unsaid between them, but the weight of the moment made it clear that they didn't need words to understand what was happening.

"I'll stay by your side," Lucas said, stepping closer, his voice filled with determination. "Whatever you decide to do next, I'll be there."

Elena's chest tightened, her emotions swirling with gratitude and sorrow. She had feared losing him, but he was still here, willing to stand by her even after everything had changed.

"I don't know where this path will take us," Elena admitted, her voice soft.

Lucas reached out and took her hand, his grip warm and steady. "Then we'll find out together."

For the first time in what felt like an eternity, Elena allowed herself to breathe. The curse, the hunger, the centuries-old battle—it was all behind her now. The future stretched before her, wide and full of possibility, and she wasn't walking into it alone.

Together, they left the clearing behind, the past fading into the distance as they walked toward the dawn of a new era.

Chapter 36: The World Rebuilds

A week had passed since Elena broke the curse. The days blurred together, and the air around Sinclair Manor was thick with an uneasy calm. Life had moved forward, but the world felt different, reshaped by the events of the past few weeks. The supernatural balance that had governed the vampire factions had shifted, and though the immediate danger had passed, the weight of Elena's transformation loomed over everything.

Inside the manor, Elena stood by a window, staring out at the sprawling, untamed grounds. The power she had absorbed still coursed through her, but it no longer felt like something foreign—no longer a curse. It was her own, a new part of her identity, yet it brought with it a profound sense of responsibility.

"I don't know what comes next," Elena murmured under her breath, her thoughts drifting as she traced the pattern of raindrops on the windowpane. The world had changed, and she had changed with it, but that left more questions than answers.

"Elena."

She turned at the sound of Lucas's voice. He entered the room quietly, his presence steady and reassuring, yet she could sense the underlying tension in his posture. He had been by her side through every trial, every decision, but the shift in their dynamic was palpable. The power she now held had drawn a line between them—a line neither of them knew how to cross.

"How are you holding up?" Lucas asked, though the concern in his voice made it clear that he was more worried about her than she was letting on.

Elena offered him a small smile, though it didn't reach her eyes. "I'm... adjusting. But it's hard to know what that even means anymore."

Lucas stepped closer; his gaze unwavering. "You're different, but you're still you. That hasn't changed."

Elena nodded, grateful for his words, but deep down, she couldn't shake the feeling that her old self—the person she had been before the curse had consumed her—was fading. She had embraced the power to survive, to end the cycle that had haunted her family, but now she was something else. The old Elena, the one who had been afraid of the darkness, was gone.

"There's more happening than just my transformation," she said, turning her gaze back to the window. "The factions… the vampire world… it's all in chaos. Sebastian's death didn't end the power struggle. If anything, it's made things worse."

Lucas nodded; his expression grim. "I've heard the same. Without Sebastian and the Elder Vampire, there's a vacuum. The factions are fighting among themselves to take control, and there's no clear leader."

Elena sighed; her shoulders heavy with the weight of the political turmoil. She had never wanted to be part of the vampire world, but now, by breaking the curse, she had become its focal point.

"I don't know if I'm ready to lead them," she admitted, her voice barely above a whisper.

Lucas reached out and gently placed a hand on her arm, his touch grounding her. "You don't have to lead them. You just need to figure out what's best for you. The rest will follow."

Elena glanced up at him, her heart aching at the simplicity of his words. Lucas always made it sound so easy, but the truth was far more complicated. The power inside her, the remnants of the curse—it had changed her. She wasn't just Elena Sinclair anymore. She was something more, something that the vampire world would either rally behind or seek to destroy.

Chapter 37: The Consequences of Power

Later that evening, Elena stood in the study, flipping through the pages of her father's journals once again. The books that had once been filled with desperation and fear now seemed like relics of a past she had left behind. The curse had been her father's obsession, the reason for his downfall. But now, she saw the curse for what it truly was—a key, not to control, but to transformation.

A knock on the door broke her concentration, and when she turned, Isolde stood in the doorway.

"Elena," Isolde greeted her, stepping into the room with a nod of acknowledgment. "I've just returned from the city. There's been a shift in the factions."

Elena closed the journal, her brow furrowing. "A shift?"

Isolde nodded; her expression serious. "With the Elder Vampire and Sebastian gone, the factions are scrambling for leadership. Some see you as the rightful heir to that power, while others…" Her voice trailed off, a shadow passing over her face. "Others believe that what you've done has destabilized the entire system. They want to take you down before you become a threat."

Elena's chest tightened. She had expected resistance, but hearing it spoken aloud made it feel more real. "They think I'll try to take control of them."

"They fear what they don't understand," Isolde said. "You're an unknown. You've broken the curse, something no one thought possible, and now you're something they've never seen before. That makes you dangerous in their eyes."

Elena's gaze hardened. "I didn't break the curse to take over. I did it to end the cycle."

Isolde nodded, her expression softening. "I know that. But power shifts rarely happen peacefully. There are those who see you as a threat to the status quo, and they will act accordingly."

Elena turned away, pacing the room as her mind raced. She hadn't asked for this power, but now it was hers. And with it came responsibilities—ones that extended beyond her personal struggle with the curse.

"What do I do?" she asked, her voice quieter now, the weight of the situation settling over her.

Isolde hesitated, then spoke with measured certainty. "You need to decide what kind of future you want for yourself—and for them. The vampires are leaderless, lost in their own struggles. They need someone to guide them, whether they know it or not. That could be you."

Elena's heart pounded. "But I don't want that."

"I know," Isolde said gently. "But sometimes, the role we're meant to play isn't the one we choose. You've already changed the game. Now you have to decide whether to let it play out or take control of it."

Elena stood in silence, the enormity of the decision pressing down on her. She could walk away from it all, retreat into the quiet life she had once dreamed of. But that life was gone, and the vampire world was in chaos. If she did nothing, it could spiral out of control. But if she stepped forward, if she took on the mantle of leadership… she risked becoming something she had always feared.

After a long moment, she turned to Isolde, her eyes filled with a quiet resolve. "I'm not ready to lead them. But I can't ignore what's happening, either. If I don't act, more people—more vampires—will die in the struggle."

Isolde's lips curved into a small smile, though it didn't reach her eyes. "Then it's time to face them. Show them what you've become."

Chapter 38: A Reckoning

The following day, Elena stood at the center of a vast underground chamber—the headquarters of the Sanguis Ascendancy, one of the most powerful vampire factions. The chamber was filled with vampires, all of them watching her with a mixture of curiosity and suspicion. She could feel their eyes on her, their unspoken questions hanging in the air like a storm about to break.

At the head of the room stood Adrian, the leader of the Ascendancy. He was tall and imposing, with a cold, calculating gaze that seemed to pierce through her. He had called this meeting in response to the power vacuum left by the deaths of the Elder Vampire and Sebastian, and now Elena was at the center of it.

"Why have you come here, Elena Sinclair?" Adrian asked, his voice echoing through the chamber. "You've broken the curse, yes. But now the vampire world is in chaos. What do you intend to do about it?"

Elena stood tall, her heart pounding in her chest. She could feel the power inside her, the remnants of the curse that had transformed her, and though it was still new to her, she knew she couldn't shy away from it now.

"I came here because I want to stop the bloodshed," Elena said, her voice strong and steady. "I know you're all fighting for control, but the truth is, the old ways are gone. The curse is broken. The power you've been fighting over doesn't exist anymore."

Murmurs spread through the crowd, some vampires casting skeptical glances at each other, others openly hostile. Adrian's expression remained impassive, but his eyes gleamed with interest.

"And what would you have us do, Elena?" Adrian asked, his tone bordering on mocking. "Surrender to you?"

"I don't want you to surrender," Elena replied, her gaze unwavering. "But I'm not going to stand by while you tear each other apart. There's a new way forward, and it starts with understanding that the power you've been chasing is gone. If you want to survive, you'll need to adapt."

Adrian's lips curled into a faint smile. "Adapt, you say? And what would that look like?"

Elena took a deep breath, her mind racing. She hadn't come here with a plan, but now, standing before them, she knew she had to offer them something—something that would keep them from descending into chaos.

"I'm offering you a chance to build something new," Elena said, her voice calm but firm. "The vampire world doesn't have to be governed by blood and power anymore. We can create a new system—one where vampires can exist without constant fear of destruction."

Adrian arched an eyebrow. "A utopia, then?"

"Not a utopia," Elena corrected. "But a future where we don't have to keep fighting each other."

The room fell silent, the weight of her words hanging in the air. Some of the vampires seemed intrigued, while others remained skeptical. But Adrian, for all his coldness, seemed to be considering her proposal.

"You speak of change, Elena Sinclair," he said slowly. "But change is dangerous. It threatens everything we've built. What makes you think the vampire world will accept it?"

Elena's gaze hardened. "Because if you don't change, you'll destroy yourselves."

Adrian studied her for a long moment, then gave a slight nod of acknowledgment. "Perhaps. But change doesn't happen overnight."

"I'm not asking for overnight," Elena said. "I'm asking for a beginning."

The room remained tense, but the tide was shifting. Elena could feel it. The old ways were dying, and though the vampires in the room might not have fully accepted it yet, they were beginning to see the truth. The curse had been the foundation of their world, and now that it was gone, they had no choice but to evolve.

After a long silence, Adrian stepped forward, his gaze locking with Elena's. "You've made your point, Elena. But the vampire world won't change without resistance. There will be those who will challenge you, who will see you as a threat to the way things have always been."

Elena nodded, her resolve unshaken. "I know. But I'm ready for them."

Adrian gave a faint smile, and for the first time, there was a flicker of respect in his eyes. "Very well. Let's see what kind of future you can build."

Chapter 38: The Weight of Leadership

As the meeting dispersed, Elena walked through the halls of the underground chamber, her thoughts heavy with the burden she had taken on. She had spoken of change, of building a new future for the vampire world, but the reality of that task was far more daunting than the words she had spoken.

Lucas was waiting for her as she stepped outside into the cold night air, his expression unreadable.

"How did it go?" he asked quietly.

Elena shook her head, unsure how to answer. "It's not over yet. They're willing to listen, but I don't know if they'll follow."

Lucas stepped closer, his hand finding hers. "You gave them something to think about. That's more than they've had in a long time."

Elena sighed, her shoulders sagging under the weight of the responsibility she had taken on. "I didn't ask for this. I didn't want to lead them."

"I know," Lucas said gently. "But you're the only one who can."

Elena met his gaze, her heart heavy with the truth of his words. She had fought to break the curse, to free herself from its grip, but now she found herself at the center of a new struggle—a struggle to rebuild a world that had been shaped by darkness for centuries.

"I don't know if I'm strong enough," she whispered.

Lucas squeezed her hand, his voice steady. "You are. You've come this far. You've survived everything they've thrown at you. You can do this."

Elena took a deep breath, letting his words wash over her. She had never wanted power, never wanted to lead. But now that the curse was broken, she was the one with the ability to reshape the future—not just for herself, but for the entire vampire world.

"I'm not going to be the same person I was," she said softly, her voice filled with both fear and acceptance.

"I know," Lucas said, his gaze unwavering. "And I'll be with you, no matter who you become."

Elena closed her eyes, feeling the weight of the moment settle over her. She had broken the curse, but the true battle was just beginning. The vampire world was in turmoil, and she would have to fight to create the future she envisioned. But with Lucas by her side, she knew she wasn't facing it alone.

As the wind whispered through the trees, Elena opened her eyes and looked out at the dark horizon. The future was uncertain, full of danger and possibility, but for the first time, she felt ready to face it.

Whatever came next, she would be the one to decide her fate.

Chapter 39: A New Threat

As the days passed, Elena worked tirelessly to establish the foundations of the new order she had promised. The vampire factions were fractured, their power struggles fierce and deeply rooted, but Elena had made her intentions clear: the old ways were over, and a new future was on the horizon.

But even as she focused on rebuilding, a new threat began to emerge—one that she hadn't anticipated.

It started with whispers. Rumors of a powerful, ancient force stirring in the shadows. A name that hadn't been spoken in centuries: **The Firstborn**.

Elena first heard the rumors from Isolde, who had returned from a reconnaissance mission in one of the smaller vampire enclaves. The fear in Isolde's eyes had been unmistakable.

"The Firstborn is more than a myth," Isolde had told her, her voice trembling. "It's a vampire older than any of us, older than the Elder Vampire. And now, it's waking."

Elena's blood ran cold at the thought. She had broken the curse, but in doing so, had she awoken something even more dangerous?

"We don't know what it wants," Isolde continued. "But if it's true—if the Firstborn is returning—it could mean the end of everything."

Elena's heart pounded in her chest as the weight of Isolde's words settled over her. The power she had unleashed by breaking the curse had shifted the balance of the supernatural world, and now something far older, far more dangerous, was stirring.

"We need to find out more," Elena said, her voice steady despite the fear gnawing at her insides. "If the Firstborn is real, we need to know what we're up against."

Isolde nodded; her expression grim. "I'll reach out to my contacts. We don't have much time."

As Isolde left to begin her search, Elena stood in the center of the room, her mind racing. She had thought breaking the curse would be the end of her struggle, but now she realized it had only been the beginning. A new threat was rising—one that could destroy everything for which she had fought.

Elena clenched her fists, her resolve hardening. She had survived the curse. She had survived Sebastian. And now, she would survive this.

No matter what the future held, she would face it head-on.

Chapter 40: Faction Politics

Elena stood in the grand hall of the Sanguis Ascendancy's headquarters, her gaze sweeping over the assembled leaders of the various vampire factions. The room was filled with tension—an undercurrent of distrust that made the air feel thick and suffocating. She had called this meeting to address the growing instability in the vampire world, but as she looked around, it was clear that not everyone was willing to listen.

Adrian, the leader of the Ascendancy, sat at the head of the table, his eyes fixed on Elena. To his left was **Maris**, a shrewd and calculating vampire who led the **Nightborn Syndicate**, a faction known for its ruthless tactics and secretive nature. On the other side of the table sat **Varek**, the leader of the **Order of the Forgotten**, a faction that prided itself on its connection to ancient vampire traditions and rituals.

They were all here because they knew the balance of power had shifted. The curse had been broken, but in its wake, the vampire world had been thrown into chaos. Factions were vying for control, and without a central figure to unite them, the threat of war loomed large.

"We need to stop pretending that the old ways will save us," Elena said, her voice steady as she addressed the room. "The curse is gone, and with it, the power structure that's governed the vampire world for centuries. If we don't adapt, we'll destroy ourselves."

Maris's sharp eyes narrowed as she leaned forward. "And what, exactly, do you propose? That we simply follow you. An outsider who broke the very curse that kept us in check?"

Elena met her gaze, unflinching. "I didn't come here to seize control. I came here to offer a way forward—a future where we don't have to keep fighting each other for power."

Varek scoffed; his expression filled with disdain. "You think you can end centuries of tradition with a few words? The vampire world thrives on power. It's what sustains us, what keeps order. Without it, we're nothing."

Elena took a deep breath, keeping her voice calm but firm. "I'm not asking you to abandon your power. I'm asking you to think beyond the old ways. The curse was a tool to control us, to keep us in line. Now that it's gone, we have a chance to create something new—something better."

Adrian watched the exchange with a calculating gaze, his fingers steepled beneath his chin. "You speak of change, Elena, but change breeds instability. And instability leads to war. If you want us to follow your vision, you'll need to prove that it won't tear us apart."

Elena's jaw tightened. "The vampire world is already tearing itself apart. But if we keep clinging to the old ways, we'll be fighting a war that none of us can win."

Maris's lips curled into a sly smile. "And who says we can't win? Power has always been the currency of the vampire world. Those who have it will survive. Those who don't… well, they're expendable."

The room fell into a tense silence as Elena considered her next move. She knew that Maris and Varek represented the old guard—the vampires who had built their empires on the foundations of the curse. They weren't interested in change. They were interested in maintaining control, no matter the cost.

But Elena also knew that there were others in the room who were tired of the constant power struggles. Vampires who had seen the damage done by the curse and wanted something different. She had to find a way to reach them—to show them that there was another path.

"I'm not here to take your power," Elena said, her voice strong. "I'm here to offer a way to use it for something more than just survival. The vampire world doesn't have to be defined by fear and bloodshed. We can build something new—together."

Adrian's gaze flicked between Maris and Varek, then back to Elena. "What exactly are you proposing?"

Elena took a deep breath, knowing that this was the moment that would define her future—and the future of the vampire world. "A council. A unified leadership that represents all factions. Each of you would have a voice, but no one would hold absolute power. Decisions would be made collectively, for the good of all."

The room erupted into murmurs, some vampires nodding in approval, while others looked skeptical. Varek sneered, his voice dripping with disdain. "A council? That sounds like weakness. We're vampires, not humans. We thrive on strength, not consensus."

Maris smirked. "And what makes you think we can trust each other enough to form such a council? Vampires are not known for their loyalty."

Elena met their doubts head-on. "That's exactly why we need a council. The old ways are failing. If we don't adapt, we'll destroy ourselves."

Adrian sat back in his chair, his eyes narrowing as he studied Elena. "It's an ambitious idea. But ambition without results is meaningless. How do we know you can keep this fragile peace from collapsing?"

Elena held his gaze, her voice unwavering. "Because I'm not fighting for power. I'm fighting for survival—for all of us."

Adrian's lips curled into a faint smile. "Very well. Let's see if your vision holds up under pressure. But be warned, Elena—if you fail, the consequences will be dire."

Chapter 41: Lucas's Internal Struggle

After the tense meeting with the vampire leaders, Elena and Lucas returned to the safety of Sinclair Manor. The weight of what had transpired hung heavily between them, and as they walked through the silent corridors, Lucas could feel the distance growing between them.

He had always believed in Elena, but the more she stepped into this new role—this position of leadership and power—the more he felt like he was losing her. She wasn't the same person she had been when this all started, and while he understood that change was inevitable, it didn't make it any easier.

"Elena," Lucas began, his voice hesitant as they entered the library. "Do you think this is what you really want?"

Elena turned to face him; her expression soft but filled with resolve. "I don't know if it's what I want. But I know it's what I have to do."

Lucas frowned, his heart tightening at her words. "But what about us? What about everything we've been through together? I can feel you slipping away, and I'm afraid that if you keep going down this path… I'll lose you."

Elena's gaze softened, and she stepped closer to him, placing a hand on his arm. "You won't lose me, Lucas. I'm still here."

"But for how long?" Lucas asked, his voice strained. "You're becoming something else, Elena. Something more powerful than any of us could have imagined. And I don't know if I can keep up with that."

Elena's heart ached at the pain in his voice, and for a moment, she felt the weight of her choices crashing down on her. She had been so focused on ending the curse, on stopping the endless cycle of bloodshed, that she hadn't fully considered the toll it was taking on her relationships—on Lucas.

"I never wanted this," Elena said quietly. "I never asked for the curse, or the power, or any of it. But now that I have it, I have to find a way to use it for good. I have to stop the vampire world from tearing itself apart."

Lucas's expression softened, and he reached out to take her hand in his. "I know. And I'm proud of you for everything you've done. But I'm scared, Elena. I'm scared of what this is doing to us."

Elena's heart clenched as she looked into his eyes, seeing the love and fear that mirrored her own. She had been so focused on her responsibilities that she hadn't realized how much it was affecting the person she cared about most.

"I don't want to lose you either," Elena whispered, her voice trembling. "But I don't know how to be both—how to be the leader they need and still be the person you fell in love with."

Lucas sighed, pulling her into his arms. "Maybe you don't have to be both. Maybe you just need to be yourself."

Elena rested her head against his chest, feeling the warmth of his embrace. For the first time in days, she allowed herself to relax, to let go of the weight she had been carrying.

"I'll always be here for you, Elena," Lucas said softly. "No matter what happens."

Elena closed her eyes, letting his words wash over her. She knew that the road ahead was uncertain, filled with challenges she couldn't yet foresee. But as long as Lucas was by her side, she knew she could face whatever came next.

Chapter 41: The Rise of the Firstborn

Days passed, and while the vampire factions cautiously entertained Elena's idea of a council, new whispers began to circulate through the supernatural world. Whispers of an ancient power—one that predated the Elder Vampire, one that had been sleeping for centuries.

The Firstborn.

Elena had first heard the name in passing, but as the days went on, the rumors grew more insistent. The Firstborn was more than just a legend—it was real. And now, it was waking.

Isolde had been the first to bring back concrete information. She had traveled to the farthest reaches of the vampire world, speaking with ancient vampires who still remembered the time before the curse. The stories they told were chilling.

"The Firstborn isn't like any vampire we've encountered," Isolde explained one evening as she sat across from Elena in the manor's study. "It's older, more powerful. It predates the bloodlines that we know. Some say it's the progenitor of all vampires—a creature born from the union of darkness and blood."

Elena frowned, her fingers tightening around the armrest of her chair. "And now it's waking up?"

Isolde nodded, her expression grim. "The breaking of the curse, the power shift—it's disturbed the balance. The Firstborn has been sleeping for centuries, but now, it's sensing the changes in the supernatural world. And it's stirring."

Elena's heart pounded in her chest. She had thought breaking the curse would be the end of her battle, but now it seemed she had only unlocked a new, far more dangerous threat.

"What does it want?" Elena asked, her voice quiet.

Isolde's eyes darkened. "Power. Control. And it will stop at nothing to reclaim its place at the top of the vampire hierarchy."

Elena stood from her chair, pacing the room as her mind raced. The Firstborn was older and more powerful than any vampire she had encountered, and the thought of facing such a creature was terrifying.

But she couldn't back down now.

"We need to find it before it finds us," Elena said, her voice filled with determination. "If the Firstborn is as powerful as they say, then it could undo everything we've fought for."

Isolde stood as well, her gaze steady. "I'll gather more information. There are still vampires who might know where the Firstborn's resting place is. But we don't have much time."

Elena nodded, her mind already turning to the preparations they would need to make. The Firstborn was coming, and when it arrived, it would bring with it a level of destruction they had never seen before.

But Elena had faced the curse, faced the Elder Vampire, and survived. She had broken the cycle, and now, she would have to find a way to stop the Firstborn—before it was too late.

Chapter 42: A New Alliance

The days that followed were a blur of strategy and preparation. Elena worked tirelessly, reaching out to the vampire factions and forming fragile alliances in the face of the looming threat. The factions were wary, but the rumors of the Firstborn's awakening were enough to unite even the most reluctant leaders.

Adrian, Maris, and Varek were the first to pledge their support, though their motivations varied. Adrian saw the Firstborn as a threat to the Ascendancy's power, while Maris and Varek understood the danger of an ancient vampire returning to reclaim dominance.

But it wasn't enough. Elena knew that if they were to stand any chance against the Firstborn, they would need more than just alliances. They would need something—or someone—who could match the Firstborn's power.

And that's when the letter arrived.

It came late one night, delivered by a messenger whose face was hidden beneath a heavy cloak. The letter was sealed with a symbol Elena didn't recognize—an ancient crest that seemed to pulse with a faint, otherworldly energy.

She opened it carefully, her heart pounding as she read the words scrawled across the page:

To Elena Sinclair, curse-breaker and keeper of the balance.

You seek to stop the rise of the Firstborn. I can help you. But know that my price will be steep, for I am not one who gives lightly.

Come to the Valley of Shadows, and we will speak.

—Azrael, the Watcher of the Lost.

Elena's blood ran cold at the name. Azrael was a figure spoken of only in hushed whispers, a vampire so ancient and powerful that even the factions feared him. He was said to be a guardian of secrets, a keeper of lost knowledge—and a being who had no allegiance to anyone but himself.

But if anyone knew how to stop the Firstborn, it would be him.

Chapter 43: The Watcher of the Lost

The journey to the **Valley of Shadows** was long and treacherous, the landscape shifting from dense forests to jagged cliffs that seemed to claw at the sky. The air grew colder as Elena, Lucas, and Isolde made their way deeper into the valley, the terrain growing more desolate with each step. The land itself felt cursed, untouched by time and thick with an oppressive energy that pressed down on them like a living force.

Elena's thoughts were heavy with the weight of what was to come. They were seeking out Azrael, a vampire so old that even the most ancient of the factions spoke of him in whispers. He had lived in isolation for centuries, guarding secrets no one else knew. And now, he had called for her. She didn't know what to expect, but she understood one thing clearly—this meeting would change everything.

"This place..." Lucas muttered; his voice tight with unease. "It feels wrong."

Elena glanced over at him, her gaze softening. He had been quiet for most of the journey, his concern for her growing as they ventured further into the unknown. She could feel the tension between them—an unspoken worry that whatever they found in the Valley of Shadows would only pull them further apart.

"It's ancient," Isolde said from ahead, her sharp eyes scanning the horizon. "This land has seen things we can't even begin to understand."

Elena nodded, her pulse quickening as they approached a narrow path carved into the side of a cliff. At the top of the path stood a structure—an old, crumbling fortress that looked like it had been abandoned for centuries. But Elena could feel it—the pulse of magic that radiated from the stones, ancient and powerful.

"This must be it," Elena murmured, her gaze fixed on the fortress.

As they climbed the path and approached the entrance, they were met by a figure standing at the threshold. Cloaked in shadows, the figure stepped forward, revealing a face both striking and unsettling. His eyes were a pale, glowing silver, and his skin looked like it hadn't seen sunlight in eons.

"Azrael," Isolde whispered, her voice barely audible.

Azrael's gaze fixed on Elena; his expression unreadable. "You've come."

Elena swallowed hard, stepping forward. "You called me."

Azrael nodded once, his voice low and smooth. "Yes. There are few left who could wield the power you now hold. Fewer still who could survive what you have endured."

Elena's breath caught. "You know about the curse?"

"I know everything about the curse," Azrael replied, his eyes narrowing. "It was never meant to be broken. It was meant to serve as a seal, keeping things in balance. But you—" His gaze pierced into her. "You've torn that balance apart."

Elena's chest tightened. "I had no choice. The curse was destroying me."

"And now you are bound to something greater," Azrael said, his voice heavy with meaning. "The Firstborn has been waiting for this moment, for the curse to be broken. And now that it is free, it will rise again. It will take back the power it once had, and it will seek to dominate all who oppose it."

Elena's heart pounded. "That's why I'm here. I need to know how to stop it."

Azrael's pale lips curved into a faint smile, though there was no warmth in it. "Stop it? You cannot stop what was meant to be. The Firstborn is a force beyond your comprehension."

Elena clenched her fists, frustration building inside her. "There has to be a way. There's always a way."

Azrael's smile faded, and he stepped closer to her, his silver eyes gleaming with an intensity that made her feel as though he could see through to her very soul. "Perhaps. But to face the Firstborn, you will need more than just power. You will need knowledge—knowledge that has been lost to time."

Elena held his gaze, refusing to back down. "Then tell me what I need to know."

Azrael studied her for a long moment before turning toward the entrance of the fortress. "Follow me."

Chapter 44: The Secrets of Azrael

Inside the fortress, the air was thick with the weight of centuries-old secrets. The walls were lined with books and scrolls, artifacts that radiated a dark, otherworldly energy. Azrael led them through the winding corridors until they reached a small, dimly lit chamber. In the center of the room stood a massive stone table, its surface etched with runes that pulsed faintly with a pale light.

"This," Azrael said, gesturing to the table, "is the Codex of the Forgotten. It holds the knowledge of the first vampires—those who came before even the Elder Vampire. It is from this knowledge that the Firstborn was created."

Elena approached the table cautiously, her fingers brushing the surface of the stone. The runes glowed brighter at her touch, and a strange energy surged through her, filling her with both awe and fear.

"Why are you showing me this?" Elena asked, her voice trembling slightly.

"Because you are the only one who can use it," Azrael replied. "The power of the curse you broke still lingers within you. It has changed you, made you more than just a vampire. It has made you a vessel—a conduit for something far greater. The Firstborn will seek to reclaim that power, but you have the ability to harness it."

Elena's breath caught. "You're saying I can use the power of the curse to stop the Firstborn?"

Azrael's gaze darkened. "Yes. But the price will be high. The power you wield will come at the cost of your humanity. The more you use it, the more you will become like the Firstborn—ancient, powerful, but also distant from the world of the living."

Elena's heart pounded in her chest. She had already felt the changes within her—the growing distance between her and the life she had once known. But to lose her humanity entirely? It was a price she wasn't sure she was willing to pay.

"There must be another way," Lucas said, stepping forward, his voice filled with urgency. "Elena can't become like them."

Azrael's gaze flicked to Lucas; his expression cold. "There is no other way. The Firstborn is not a being that can be defeated by strength alone. It is a creature of pure darkness, bound to the ancient magic that gave birth to the vampire race. To fight it, you must become what it is."

Elena looked at Lucas, her heart aching at the fear in his eyes. She knew what he was thinking—that if she took this path, she would lose herself, lose everything that had made her who she was. But the alternative was worse. If she did nothing, the Firstborn would rise, and the vampire world would fall into chaos.

"I don't have a choice," Elena said softly, turning back to Azrael. "Tell me what I need to do."

Azrael nodded, his expression grave. "The Codex holds the key to unlocking the ancient power of the first vampires. But it is not a simple process. You will need to undergo a ritual—one that will bind the power to you, and in doing so, unlock the full potential of what you have become."

Elena's stomach twisted with a mixture of fear and resolve. "What kind of ritual?"

Azrael gestured to the runes on the table. "These runes will guide the process. You must offer something of great personal value—something that ties you to your humanity. Once you do, the Codex will reveal the ancient power, and it will become a part of you."

Elena's heart pounded as she considered the gravity of what Azrael was asking. To bind herself to this power, she would have to give up a piece of herself—a piece of her humanity. The thought terrified her, but she knew that if she didn't act, the Firstborn would rise and take everything from her.

"I'll do it," Elena said, her voice steady despite the fear coursing through her veins.

Lucas stepped forward; his expression filled with desperation. "Elena, wait. You don't have to do this. There has to be another way."

Elena looked at him, her heart breaking at the pain in his voice. She wished there was another way—wished she could walk away from all of this and return to the life they had once dreamed of. But that life was gone, and she couldn't turn her back on the responsibility she now carried.

"I have to, Lucas," she whispered, her voice trembling. "This is the only way to stop the Firstborn."

Lucas's hands clenched into fists at his sides, his face tight with emotion. "And what happens to you? What happens to us?"

Elena looked away, her chest tightening. She didn't have an answer. All she knew was that if she didn't do this, there wouldn't be a future for any of them.

"Prepare yourself," Azrael said, his voice cutting through the tension in the room. "Once you begin, there will be no turning back."

Elena nodded, taking a deep breath as she steeled herself for what was to come. She could feel the weight of the Codex pressing down on her, its ancient magic calling to her, beckoning her toward the power she would need to face the Firstborn.

As she stepped forward and placed her hands on the runes, the air around her seemed to shift, growing heavy with the force of the magic she was about to unleash.

And in that moment, she knew that nothing would ever be the same again.

Chapter 45: The Ritual of Sacrifice

The ritual chamber was dimly lit, the flickering glow of candles casting long, wavering shadows across the stone walls. Elena stood at the center of the room, the ancient runes of the Codex glowing faintly beneath her feet. The air was thick with magic, the power of the first vampires stirring all around her, waiting to be claimed.

Azrael stood off to the side, watching her with an unreadable expression. He had explained the ritual in detail, the steps she would need to take to bind the power to herself. It was a dangerous process, one that required more than just physical strength. It required a sacrifice—something of great personal value, something that would tether her to the ancient magic.

Elena's heart pounded in her chest as she looked down at the Codex, the weight of what she was about to do pressing down on her. She could feel the power waiting for her, calling to her, but it wasn't without cost. The more she gave herself to it, the more she would lose.

Lucas stood nearby, his face pale with worry. He hadn't spoken much since they had entered the chamber, but she could feel the tension radiating off him. He didn't want her to go through with this, but she had no choice.

"What are you going to offer?" Lucas asked, his voice tight with emotion.

Elena swallowed hard, her gaze shifting to the ring on her finger—the ring Lucas had given her when they had first realized they were in love. It was a simple thing, but it represented everything she had once dreamed of—a life with Lucas, free from the burden of the curse. A life where they could be together, without fear or darkness hanging over them.

That life was gone now.

"This," Elena said softly, holding up the ring. "It's the only thing I have left that connects me to the life I used to want."

Lucas's eyes widened, his voice trembling with emotion. "Elena, no. You don't have to—"

"I do," she interrupted, her voice steady but filled with sorrow. "If I don't do this, the Firstborn will destroy everything. This is the only way."

Lucas stepped forward; his hands clenched at his sides. "And what about us? What happens if you give this up? Will you still be you?"

Elena's heart clenched as she met his gaze, the pain in his eyes reflecting the anguish she felt in her own heart. She didn't know what would happen once the ritual was complete, didn't know how much of herself she would lose. But she couldn't turn back now.

"I don't know," she whispered, her voice breaking. "But I have to try."

Lucas's face tightened with emotion, and for a moment, he looked as though he wanted to stop her, to pull her away from the ritual and take her far from the darkness that was consuming them. But he didn't move.

Instead, he took a step back, his eyes filled with resignation. "I love you, Elena. No matter what happens."

Tears pricked at the corners of her eyes, and she nodded, her voice trembling. "I love you too."

With a deep breath, Elena stepped forward and placed the ring on the center of the Codex. The runes beneath her feet flared to life, glowing with an intense, otherworldly light that filled the chamber. The air crackled with energy as the power of the ancient vampires surged toward her, wrapping around her like a living force.

For a moment, she felt as though she was floating, weightless, suspended between worlds. The magic of the Codex poured into her, filling her with a power so vast and ancient that it threatened to consume her whole. She could feel the darkness pressing in on her, the cold tendrils of the Firstborn's magic reaching out to her, seeking to claim her as its own.

But Elena didn't back down. She stood firm, her mind focused on the task at hand. She had come here to claim the power, to use it to stop the Firstborn. And she would not be swayed.

With a scream, she let the magic flow through her, letting it reshape her, transform her. The air around her shimmered with power as the runes of the Codex burned brightly beneath her feet. She could feel the sacrifice—the loss of her humanity—slipping away from her, replaced by something else, something darker and more powerful.

The ritual was complete.

When the light faded, Elena stood at the center of the chamber, her breath coming in ragged gasps. She could feel the power inside her, pulsing with a dark, ancient energy. She had become something more than she had ever imagined—something far greater, but also far more dangerous.

Lucas stepped forward, his face filled with a mixture of awe and fear. "Elena… are you okay?"

Elena turned to him, her eyes glowing faintly with the power she had just claimed. "I'm not sure."

Lucas hesitated; his voice soft. "You're still you, right?"

Elena's heart ached at his words, but she didn't know how to answer. She could feel the change inside her, the darkness that now flowed through her veins. She was still Elena, but she was also something more—

something that had been forever altered by the power of the first vampires.

"I don't know," she whispered, her voice trembling.

Before Lucas could respond, Azrael stepped forward, his expression unreadable. "It is done. You now possess the power to face the Firstborn. But remember, this power comes at a cost. The more you use it, the more you will lose yourself to it."

Elena nodded, her mind racing with the weight of what she had just done. She had claimed the power she needed to stop the Firstborn, but at what cost?

As they left the chamber, the air around them felt heavy with the weight of the future. The Firstborn was coming, and now, Elena was the only one who could stop it.

But the question remained—would she still be herself when it was all over?

Chapter 46: The Storm on the Horizon

The days that followed were filled with a tense, uneasy calm. Elena had returned to Sinclair Manor with Lucas and Isolde, but nothing felt the same. The ritual had changed her, and though she still felt like herself, there was a lingering sense of dread that gnawed at the edges of her consciousness.

The power she had claimed from the Codex was vast, more than she had ever imagined. It flowed through her like a living force, its presence always there, whispering at the back of her mind. She had used the magic to strengthen herself, to prepare for the battle with the Firstborn, but the cost of that power weighed heavily on her soul.

Lucas had been by her side through it all, but even he could sense the distance growing between them. He hadn't said it outright, but Elena knew that he feared what the power was doing to her—that it was pulling her away from him, changing her in ways neither of them fully understood.

"I don't know what's going to happen," Elena said one evening as they stood together in the quiet of the manor's garden. The sky above them was dark, heavy with the promise of a storm.

Lucas glanced over at her; his face etched with worry. "We'll face it together. Whatever comes next, we'll get through it."

Elena smiled, but it didn't reach her eyes. "I don't know if it's that simple, Lucas. I can feel it… the power. It's growing stronger every day, and I don't know how long I can control it."

Lucas reached out, taking her hand in his. "You're stronger than you think. You can control it."

Elena squeezed his hand, her heart aching with both love and fear. She wanted to believe him, wanted to believe that she could hold onto herself, that she could keep the darkness at bay. But deep down, she wasn't sure.

As they stood in the garden, a cold wind swept through the air, rustling the leaves, and sending a shiver down Elena's spine. The storm was coming—both the literal one brewing in the sky and the one that loomed over the vampire world.

They didn't have much time.

Isolde approached from the shadows; her expression grim. "I've received word from my contacts. The Firstborn has fully awakened. It's only a matter of time before it makes its move."

Elena's stomach twisted with a mixture of fear and determination. She had known this moment was coming, but now that it was here, the weight of it pressed down on her like a crushing force.

"We need to be ready," Elena said, her voice steady despite the turmoil inside her. "This will be the fight of our lives."

Isolde nodded; her eyes hard. "We'll face it together."

As they prepared for the coming storm, Elena couldn't shake the feeling that everything was about to change. The Firstborn was a force unlike anything they had ever faced, and though she had gained the power to stand against it, the price of that power was a constant reminder of the danger she faced—not just from the Firstborn, but from herself.

The sky rumbled with the sound of distant thunder, and Elena turned her gaze to the horizon, where dark clouds gathered in ominous swirls. The storm was almost upon them, and when it hit, nothing would ever be the same.

Chapter 47: Gathering Forces

The storm rumbled ominously overhead as Elena, Lucas, and Isolde moved swiftly to prepare for the coming confrontation. Elena's mind was filled with the weight of what lay ahead—her newfound power, the ancient threat of the Firstborn, and the uncertainty of what the final battle would demand of her. The power she had taken from the Codex felt like a living thing, pressing against her, testing her limits.

The vampire factions were assembling. Word had spread quickly through the supernatural world about the Firstborn's awakening, and even those who had once fought against Elena's vision were now forced to acknowledge the severity of the threat. The **Sangu is Ascendancy**, the **Night born Syndicate**, and the **Order of the Forgotten** had each sent their strongest warriors, understanding that the only chance of survival lay in standing together.

Adrian, the leader of the Ascendancy, approached Elena as she stood in the center of Sinclair Manor's grand hall, overseeing the preparations. His expression was hard, his eyes betraying none of the uncertainty that had plagued their earlier dealings.

"We're ready," Adrian said, his voice clipped. "But don't mistake this for loyalty, Elena. We're only here because the Firstborn threatens us all."

Elena met his gaze, her voice calm but resolute. "I don't care about loyalty, Adrian. I care about survival. If we don't work together, none of us will survive this."

Adrian's lips pressed into a thin line, but he nodded, stepping back as more vampires entered the hall. Elena could see the tension in their faces, the fear that clung to the air like a fog. They all knew the stories—the ancient legends of the Firstborn, a being of unimaginable power who had once ruled over the vampire world with an iron fist.

Isolde joined Elena's side, her eyes scanning the room as more factions arrived. "They're frightened," she said quietly. "They've spent centuries in their power struggles, but now that something greater than all of them has risen, they don't know how to handle it."

"They should be frightened," Elena replied, her voice grim. "The Firstborn isn't like anything they've ever faced."

Isolde nodded, her expression serious. "But we have you. And you've proven that you're capable of more than any of them expected."

Elena sighed, her gaze drifting toward the window, where the storm clouds continued to gather in dark, swirling masses. "I just hope it's enough."

Chapter 48: The Firstborn's Awakening

Far from Sinclair Manor, deep within the shadowy ruins of an ancient fortress, the Firstborn stirred. The air around it crackled with energy, the ancient magic of the vampire world coiling around the being like a living force. Its eyes—black and bottomless—opened slowly, and for the first time in centuries, the Firstborn took a breath.

The vampire world had changed in its absence, but it mattered little. The Firstborn had waited patiently, resting in the dark, biding its time until the balance of power was shattered. And now, the curse was broken. The world had been thrown into chaos, and it was time for the Firstborn to reclaim its throne.

The shadows twisted and writhed around the Firstborn's form, the air growing colder as the creature rose from the stone altar where it had slept for centuries. Its body was sleek and predatory, its movements fluid and unnatural. Every step it took sent ripples of energy through the surrounding air, a reminder of the ancient power it held.

The Firstborn's gaze flicked to the horizon, where it could feel the stirring of the vampire factions. They were gathering—readying themselves for a battle they could never hope to win. The Firstborn smiled, a cold, cruel expression that held no warmth.

It was time.

Chapter 49: The Calm Before the Storm

Back at Sinclair Manor, the tension was palpable. The factions had gathered, their warriors preparing for what they all knew would be the greatest battle of their lives. Elena moved through the halls, offering words of encouragement where she could, but the weight of what was to come bore down on her shoulders like an oppressive force.

She hadn't seen Lucas in hours. Since the ritual, he had kept his distance, watching her from afar with a mixture of love and fear. Elena could feel the distance growing between them, could sense the fear in his eyes whenever he looked at her. She was changing, becoming something more powerful, something darker—and Lucas didn't know how to handle it.

Elena found him in the garden, standing beneath the twisted oak tree that had stood for centuries. His back was to her, his shoulders tense as he stared up at the storm clouds rolling in from the horizon.

"Lucas," Elena said softly, stepping closer to him.

He turned slowly; his eyes filled with a deep sadness. "It's almost time, isn't it?"

Elena nodded; her heart heavy. "The Firstborn will be here soon. We have to be ready."

Lucas sighed, his hands clenching into fists at his sides. "And what happens after that, Elena? What happens to us?"

Elena's chest tightened. She had asked herself the same question a hundred times, but she still didn't have an answer. The power she had taken from the Codex was changing her, pulling her further away from the life she had once imagined with Lucas. She could feel the darkness growing inside her, and though she still felt like herself, there was always a part of her that wondered how long she could hold on.

"I don't know," Elena whispered, her voice trembling. "But whatever happens, I want you to know that I love you."

Lucas's face softened, and for a moment, he looked like the man she had fallen in love with all those years ago. But there was a sadness in his eyes that wouldn't go away.

"I love you too," Lucas said, his voice tight with emotion. "But I'm afraid of what this is doing to you. Of what you're becoming."

Elena reached out, taking his hand in hers. "I'm still me, Lucas. I haven't changed that much."

Lucas shook his head, his voice barely a whisper. "Not yet. But you will."

Elena's heart ached at his words, but she knew there was truth in them. The power she had taken from the Codex was vast, ancient, and it was only a matter of time before it consumed her. But she couldn't think about that now. Not with the Firstborn so close.

"We'll talk about this after," Elena said softly, her voice filled with quiet determination. "After we've stopped the Firstborn."

Lucas nodded, though his eyes were still filled with uncertainty. "I'll fight by your side, Elena. No matter what happens."

Elena smiled, a flicker of warmth breaking through the storm of emotions swirling inside her. "I wouldn't want it any other way."

Chapter 50: The Firstborn Arrives

The sky above Sinclair Manor had grown dark, the storm clouds swirling in violent spirals as the Firstborn's presence drew closer. The air was thick with tension, every vampire in the courtyard on edge, their eyes fixed on the horizon.

Elena stood at the head of the gathered factions, her heart pounding in her chest as she felt the approaching darkness. The power she had taken from the Codex surged within her, ready to be unleashed, but she knew that once the battle began, there would be no turning back.

The Firstborn was coming.

"They're almost here," Isolde said quietly, her gaze fixed on the distant treeline. "You can feel it, can't you?"

Elena nodded, her body tensing as the shadows in the forest began to shift. The air grew colder, and a strange silence fell over the courtyard as the first figure emerged from the trees.

The Firstborn.

It moved like a shadow, its form barely visible in the darkness, but the power it radiated was unmistakable. Every step it took sent ripples of energy through the air, the ground beneath its feet trembling with the force of its presence.

Behind the Firstborn, a legion of ancient vampires emerged from the shadows, their eyes glowing with a cold, predatory hunger. They were the Firstborn's army, vampires who had once served it in the ancient days of the vampire world, now resurrected to fight once more.

Elena's heart pounded as she stepped forward, her eyes locked on the Firstborn's shadowy form. This was it—the battle they had been preparing for. The fight that would decide the future of the vampire world.

The Firstborn stopped at the edge of the courtyard, its gaze sweeping over the assembled factions. When it spoke, its voice was low and cold, reverberating through the air like a distant thunder.

"You dare to stand against me?"

Elena clenched her fists, the power inside her surging to the surface. "We do."

The Firstborn's lips curled into a cruel smile. "You are nothing but insects, squabbling over scraps of power you do not understand. I was here before your kind even knew what power was. And now, I will reclaim what is mine."

Elena's body tensed as the Firstborn's magic pressed against her, its dark energy wrapping around her like a vise. She could feel the weight of its ancient power, the darkness that had shaped the vampire world for centuries. But she wasn't afraid.

She had faced the curse. She had broken it. And now, she would face the Firstborn.

With a scream of defiance, Elena unleashed the power she had taken from the Codex, the dark magic surging through her as she stepped forward to meet the Firstborn head-on. The air crackled with energy as the two forces collided, the ground shaking beneath their feet as the battle for the future of the vampire world began.

Chapter 51: Clash of Titans

The battle erupted with a ferocity that none of them had expected. Elena's power clashed with the Firstborn's ancient magic, the two forces colliding in a burst of energy that sent shockwaves through the air. The ground beneath them cracked and splintered, and the sky above rumbled with the force of the storm.

The vampires who had gathered to fight the Firstborn's army surged forward, their weapons drawn as they met the ancient vampires in combat. The courtyard was filled with the sounds of clashing steel, the snarls of vampires locked in battle, and the crackling of magic as spells were cast and deflected.

Elena's entire body thrummed with the power she had taken from the Codex, her mind focused on one thing: stopping the Firstborn. The ancient vampire moved with an unnatural speed, its shadowy form darting around her like a predator stalking its prey.

"You cannot defeat me," the Firstborn hissed, its voice echoing in Elena's mind. "You are a child, playing with power you do not understand."

Elena's jaw clenched as she swung her hand, releasing a burst of dark energy that slammed into the Firstborn, forcing it back. "I understand enough to know that your time is over."

The Firstborn let out a low, menacing laugh, its shadowy form shifting and warping as it moved closer. "Foolish girl. You think you can stand against the first of our kind? I am power incarnate. I am the darkness from which all vampires were born."

Elena's heart pounded, her mind racing as she fought to keep the Firstborn at bay. She could feel the strain of the battle weighing on her, the power she had claimed from the Codex pushing her to her limits. But she couldn't give in. Not now.

With a scream of defiance, Elena unleashed another wave of dark magic, the air around her crackling with energy as the two forces collided once more. The Firstborn staggered, its shadowy form flickering as the force of Elena's attack hit it full force.

But it wasn't enough.

The Firstborn's form solidified, its black eyes gleaming with a cold, cruel light as it lunged toward Elena, its claws outstretched. Elena barely had time to react as the ancient vampire's hand closed around her throat, lifting her off the ground as it snarled in her face.

"You are nothing," the Firstborn growled, its voice filled with contempt. "You are but a flicker of light in the darkness, and I am the night."

Elena struggled against the Firstborn's grip, her vision blurring as the ancient vampire's magic pressed down on her, suffocating her. She could feel the power slipping away from her, the darkness threatening to consume her whole.

But she wasn't done yet.

With a final burst of strength, Elena reached deep within herself, calling upon the last reserves of the power she had taken from the Codex. The darkness surged through her veins, filling her with a strength she hadn't known she possessed.

With a scream, Elena unleashed the full force of the magic, a wave of dark energy exploding from her body and sending the

Firstborn flying across the courtyard. The ground shook with the force of the blast, and the Firstborn's shadowy form flickered and warped as it crashed into the stone wall.

Elena fell to her knees, gasping for breath as the last of her energy drained from her body. The battle was far from over, but she had dealt a powerful blow. The Firstborn wasn't invincible.

But neither was she.

Chapter 52: The Turning Point

Elena staggered to her feet, her body trembling from the exertion of unleashing such immense power. The Firstborn had been knocked back, but she could feel the creature's presence looming just at the edge of the courtyard, waiting for the right moment to strike again.

Around her, the courtyard was a battlefield. Vampires clashed in brutal combat, their weapons ringing out against steel and bone. The ancient army of the Firstborn was relentless, their undead eyes glowing with a cold, predatory hunger. Elena's forces fought valiantly, but she could see the fear in their eyes—the growing realization that they might not survive this night.

Isolde was at the frontlines, her blade flashing in the dim light as she cut down the ancient vampires one after another. Her movements were precise and deadly, but even she was being pushed to her limits by the sheer numbers they faced.

Lucas was nearby, his face grim with determination as he fought beside the others. Every so often, his eyes flicked toward Elena, filled with concern and something else—a deeper fear, perhaps, that the battle wasn't just against the Firstborn, but against what Elena was becoming.

Elena clenched her fists, the darkness inside her pulsing with renewed strength. She could feel the Codex's power, tempting her to tap into more of it. If she allowed herself to fully embrace that magic, she knew she could decimate the Firstborn's army in an instant.

But the cost… it would be too high. She had already sacrificed so much—her humanity hanging by a thread. To give in completely would mean becoming something she had fought against her entire life. Could she walk that path and still find her way back?

As these thoughts weighed on her, the Firstborn rose from the debris where Elena had flung it. Its body shimmered and reformed, shadows pulling together to once again make it whole. The creature's gaze fixed on her, and its mouth curled into a twisted smile.

"You cannot defeat me," the Firstborn said, its voice like the hiss of a serpent. "Your power is but a flicker compared to the endless night that I am."

Elena gritted her teeth, feeling the rage well up inside her. She had heard those words before—heard the promise of doom from those who had tried to break her. But she wasn't that scared girl anymore.

"I've already beaten the curse," Elena replied, her voice low but firm. "I've faced death and worse. What makes you think I won't end you, too?"

The Firstborn laughed, a hollow sound that sent a chill through the air. "Because you fear what you must become to stop me."

Elena's heart pounded in her chest, the words striking too close to the truth. The Firstborn could see it—the conflict inside her. She was teetering on the edge, and the Firstborn knew it.

But before she could respond, a flash of silver darted through the air, striking the Firstborn in the side. The creature recoiled, its form flickering as it let out a screech of pain.

"Get away from her!" Lucas shouted, standing several feet away with a silver dagger in hand, his eyes blazing with fury.

The Firstborn turned its gaze toward him, its expression darkening. "You think a weapon like that can harm me?"

Lucas didn't flinch. "I know it can."

Before the Firstborn could retaliate, Lucas charged, his movements swift and precise. He dodged the Firstborn's outstretched claws, slashing at its shadowy form with a series of rapid strikes. Each hit made the Firstborn falter, its dark energy flickering and wavering under the assault.

But even as Lucas fought with everything he had, Elena could see that it wasn't enough. The Firstborn's strength was beyond anything they had encountered, and while Lucas's attacks slowed it down, they wouldn't be able to defeat it this way.

"I can help him," the darkness whispered inside her, seductive and tempting. "Give me control, and we will end this."

Elena's fists tightened at her sides, her mind racing. She couldn't lose Lucas—not now, not when everything was on the line. But if she gave in to the Codex's power, she risked losing herself completely.

As Lucas pressed forward, landing another blow that caused the Firstborn to stumble, Elena made her decision.

She would fight.

Not just against the Firstborn, but against the darkness that threatened to consume her.

With a surge of energy, Elena focused all of her power, calling upon the magic she had taken from the Codex but refusing to let it control her. She could feel the Codex pushing against her will, demanding more, but she held firm, allowing only what was needed.

"Lucas!" Elena shouted; her voice filled with authority. "Get clear!"

Lucas glanced back at her, his eyes wide with understanding, and quickly dodged out of the Firstborn's reach, rolling to safety as Elena stepped forward, her hands glowing with dark energy.

The Firstborn hissed, sensing the change in her, and turned its attention back to her. "You would challenge me again, child?"

Elena's eyes burned with determination. "This ends now."

With a wave of her hand, she unleashed a blast of dark energy, aimed directly at the Firstborn. The magic struck the creature with the force of a hurricane, sending it crashing into the stone wall of the courtyard. The ground trembled beneath them, and the air crackled with the raw power of the

Codex as Elena pressed forward, refusing to relent.

The Firstborn let out a roar of pain, its form flickering and fading as Elena's magic tore through it. For the first time, the ancient vampire looked weakened, vulnerable.

But it wasn't over yet.

The Firstborn gathered the shadows around it, its form shifting and expanding as it prepared to retaliate. Elena could feel the force of its power pressing against her, threatening to overwhelm her.

But she wasn't alone.

As the Firstborn rose to strike, a sudden burst of light filled the courtyard. Isolde appeared at Elena's side, her blade gleaming with magic as she plunged it into the Firstborn's shadowy form.

The creature screeched, its body writhing as the combined forces of Elena's magic and Isolde's blade took hold. The ancient vampire's power began to unravel, its dark energy dissipating into the night.

"You cannot stop me," the Firstborn growled, its voice weakening as it struggled to maintain its form. "I am eternal."

Elena's gaze hardened; her hands steady as she channeled the last of her power. "Not anymore."

With one final surge of energy, Elena and Isolde struck together, their combined forces tearing through the Firstborn's essence. The creature let out a final, piercing scream before its form dissolved into nothingness, leaving behind only a faint shimmer of darkness that quickly faded into the night.

The courtyard fell silent.

The battle was over.

Chapter 53: The Cost of Victory

The courtyard was eerily quiet in the aftermath of the battle. The Firstborn was gone, its shadowy presence erased from the world, but the toll of the fight hung heavy in the air. The vampire factions stood among the ruins of the courtyard, their faces etched with exhaustion and uncertainty. They had survived, but the victory had come at a steep cost.

Elena stood at the center of the courtyard, her body trembling from the exertion of channeling so much power. She could feel the Codex's magic pulsing inside her, but it no longer surged uncontrollably. She had managed to keep it in check, but just barely.

Lucas approached her cautiously, his face filled with a mixture of relief and concern. "Elena… are you okay?"

Elena took a deep breath, her eyes meeting his. "I think so. But I don't know how much longer I can keep this up."

Lucas's brow furrowed, his hand reaching out to steady her. "You don't have to do this alone. We'll figure it out—together."

Elena nodded, but deep down, she knew that things had changed. The power inside her wasn't something she could simply walk away from. It was a part of her now, and the more she used it, the more it threatened to consume her.

Isolde joined them, her face calm but serious. "We did it. The Firstborn is gone. But this isn't the end, Elena. There are still those in the vampire world who will see what you've become and want that power for themselves."

Elena sighed, her shoulders heavy with the weight of the future. "I know. But I'm not going to let them control me. I'm not going to become what the Firstborn was."

Isolde nodded; her eyes filled with quiet respect. "You've proven that you can resist the darkness. But the real battle is just beginning."

Elena glanced around the courtyard, taking in the faces of the vampires who had fought beside her. They had come together to face a common threat, but now that the Firstborn was gone, the old power struggles would undoubtedly resurface.

"What do we do now?" Lucas asked, his voice filled with uncertainty.

Elena looked toward the horizon, where the first light of dawn was beginning to break through the storm clouds. The world felt different—new, somehow. The curse was gone, the Firstborn defeated, but the future was still unwritten.

"We rebuild," Elena said softly, her voice steady. "And we make sure that this time, we do it right."

Chapter 54: A New Beginning

In the weeks that followed the battle, the vampire world began to rebuild itself. The factions, once divided by centuries of conflict, had come together in the face of a common enemy, and though there were still tensions, there was a sense of cautious hope that things could be different.

Elena had become a symbol of that hope—a leader who had not only broken the curse but had also stood against the Firstborn and survived. But with that power came new challenges. The vampire world was changing, and Elena found herself at the center of it all.

Sinclair Manor had become a gathering place for the factions, a place where decisions were made and alliances were forged. Adrian, Maris, and Varek had all pledged to work toward a new era of peace, though Elena knew that their ambitions would always drive them to seek more power.

Isolde remained by her side, serving as both a mentor and a friend, guiding Elena through the complexities of leadership. She had seen what the vampire world could become, and she was determined to help Elena steer it in the right direction.

But despite the progress, Elena couldn't shake the feeling that something was missing. The power she had taken from the Codex still pulsed within her, a constant reminder of the cost of victory. She had won the battle, but she had lost something in the process—something she wasn't sure she could ever get back.

One evening, as the sun set over the horizon, Elena stood in the garden, her thoughts heavy with the weight of the past few months. The garden had always been a place of peace for her, but now, it felt different—like a relic of a life that no longer existed.

Lucas joined her, his presence quiet but comforting. He hadn't spoken much about the battle, but Elena knew that he had been watching her closely, waiting for the moment when she would tell him what was really on her mind.

"Elena," Lucas said softly, his hand brushing hers. "What are you thinking about?"

Elena sighed, her gaze fixed on the darkening sky. "Everything. The Firstborn, the curse… the future. I feel like I've changed, Lucas. And I don't know if I can go back to who I was."

Lucas's brow furrowed; his eyes filled with concern. "You've been through more than anyone should ever have to face. But you're still you. I can see it."

Elena shook her head, her voice trembling. "I don't know if that's true anymore. The power inside me—it's growing stronger, and I don't know how to control it. What if I become something else?"

Lucas took her hand in his, his grip firm but gentle. "Then we'll face it together. Whatever happens, we'll figure it out."

Elena looked into his eyes, her heart aching with both love and fear. She wanted to believe him, wanted to believe that they could find a way forward together. But deep down, she knew that the power she carried would always set her apart.

"I don't want to lose myself," Elena whispered.

"You won't," Lucas said, his voice filled with quiet determination. "Because I won't let you."

Elena smiled, a flicker of warmth breaking through the storm of emotions inside her. She didn't know what the future held, but with Lucas by her side, she felt like she could face it—whatever it might be.

As the sun dipped below the horizon, Elena took a deep breath, the cool evening air filling her lungs. The world had changed, and so had she. But there was still hope. There was still a future.

And this time, she would be the one to shape it.

The End

Table of contents

Page 2 The Return/ chapter 1

Page 8 / chapter 2 Shadows of the Past

Page 13: chapter 3: The Awaken

Page 24 / chapter 4 The Hunger

Page 25 / chapter 5 The Aftermath

Page 29 / chapter 6: Dark Temptations

Page 39 / chapter 7: Fractured

Page 42 / chapter 8: The Hunger

Page 44 / chapter 9: The First Step

Page 48 / chapter 10: The Hunger Returns

Page 51 / chapter 11: Into the Night

Page 56 / chapter 12: The Encounter

Page 64 / chapter13: A Dangerous Place

Page 67 / chapter14:: Into The Darkness

Page 78 / chapter15: Blood and Secrets

Page 93 / chapter16: Return to the Manor

Page 97 / chapter17: The Price of Freedom

Page 103 / chapter18: Shadows Coming In

Page 111 / chapter19: The Ritual Begins

Page 113 / chapter20: The Unraveling

Page 124 / chapter 21: The Ascension

Page 127 / chapter22: Reperoussions

Page 132/ chapter 23: The Hunt Begins

Page 140/ chapter 24: A New Dawn

Page 142/ chapter 25:

Page 147/ chapter 26: Echoes of the ancestors.

Page 151/ chapter 27: Fracture of Time

Page 156/ chapter 28: the Factions awaking

Page 158/ chapter29: The Council of Shadows

Page 168 / chapter 30: Lucan's Dilemma

Page 172/ chapter 31: The Journey

Page 176 / chapter 32: The journey Begins

Page 179/ chapter 33: A Place of Power

Page 186 / chapter 34: The Final Confrontation

Page 191/ chapter 35: The New Dawn

Page 196 / chapter 36: The World Rebuilds

Page 200/ chapter 37: The Consequences of Power

Page 211/ chapter 38: The Weight of Leadership

Page 215/ chapter 39: A New Threat

Page 218/ chapter 40: Faction Politics

Page 229/ chapter 41: The Rise of the Firstborn

Page 233/ chapter 42: A New Alliance

Page 236/ chapter 43: The Watcher of the Lost

Page 241/ chapter 44: The Secrets of Azrael

Page 248/ chapter 45: The Ritual Of Sacrifice

Page 256/ chapter46: The Storm on the Horizon

Page 260/ chapter 47: Gathering Forces

Page 264 / chapter 48: The Firstborn Awaking

Page 266/ chapter 49: The Calm Before the Storm

Page 270/ chapter 50: The Firstborn Arrives

Page 274/ chapter 51: Clash of Titans

Page 279/ chapter 52: The Turning Point

Page 288/ chapter 53: The cost of Victory

Page 291/ chapter 54: A New Beginning

Made in the USA
Columbia, SC
11 October 2024

44202621R00165